The Secret Teller

Jessica Grundy

ISBN: 9781099877056

DEDICATION

I want to dedicate this book to those who thought I was finished after my first book.

CONTENTS

ACKNOWLEDGMENTS

I'd like to thank my Launch Team- Sean Thomas, Alesia McFarland, Bianca Strickland, Cari Bradley, and Shea Langford- for always pushing me to keep working on my books, for telling everyone about my books, and hyping me up when I need it. Special thank you to my boyfriend, Jeremie, for helping with formatting and all the constant encouragement. A big thank you to my editor, Christina Kaye, for being such a joy to work with and an amazing editor. The biggest thank you to my cover art designer, Erika Klassen-Green, for always taking my ideas and making the best book covers.

PROLOUGE

Chadwick pulled into his driveway, turned the car off, and just sat there. He knew his fate had been sealed; he just wasn't ready. Mustering up the courage, he slid out of his car, and walked inside, going over what he was going to say in his head. Aside from getting the news, telling his best friend was the hardest thing he'd ever had to do.

"Chadwick, what...what does this mean?"

"I'm dying Eevee. I don't have long to live."

"The doctors can't do anything? Anything at all?"

"No, they can't," Chadwick said, defeated. "I could try seeing a urologist or oncologist, but I waited too long, unfortunately."

"Are you in pain? Are you scared?" questioned Eevee.

"I'm not in a lot of pain. It's just more of being uncomfortable because I feel like I always must use the restroom. I'm not scared of dying, exactly. Everyone dies. I'm scared of what I'm leaving behind. I'm scared of leaving you. Who will look out for you once I'm gone? Who will take care of you?"

"You could give me to your brother, I guess."

Chadwick shook his head. "No, that won't work. He will just destroy you."

Chadwick paced around the dimly lit room, running his hand through his thinning hair.

"Is it insensitive of me to say I don't want to be destroyed?"

"Not at all, Eevee. My family... they just don't understand you like I do. They don't understand us. We need to find someone who will. That is my dying wish: find someone to become your new keeper."

"I can search to see who best fits the features you would like."

"Good, then I will put it in my Will that my house goes to that person. This prostate cancer is claiming my life, but I won't let it kill you, too. I worked way too hard to create you just how I wanted. I'm not just going to lay there dying knowing you are dying with me."

CHAPTER ONE

Blair sat in the backseat both angry and excited. Angry because her parents still treated her like she was a kid; she was going to be thirteen in two months. Her parents were going out of town on a business meeting and decided to tie in a vacation for their anniversary since her best friend Claire's parents said she could stay with them. She was always on her best behavior when it came to her parents work stuff. They themselves even said she was one of the most well-behaved children they had ever seen; which is why she was upset they wouldn't let her go with them.

"Sweetheart, this just isn't a place for children. Yes, your father and I know you would be on your best behavior, but you'd be in the hotel room alone most of the time. Besides, you're going to have way more fun with Claire," reassured Kimberly.

Her mom was right, she and Claire would have a really great time. They have been best friends for as long as either one of them could remember. Their dads had worked together. Their moms became best friends when Claire's dad passed away when they were babies. The two families have been close ever since. Blair realized her excitement outweighed her anger when they pulled into Claire's driveway.

Grabbing her bag, she quickly ran up and knocked on the door. When Charlie, Claire's stepbrother, opened the door, Blair's heart skipped a beat. She hadn't gotten to know him yet, but Claire always told her awful things about him. Seeing him standing there with his carrot red hair, face full of freckles, and that sinister smile sent chills running up her arms. Luckily, her mom walked up behind her so she wouldn't have to speak to him.

"Oh, hey, Charlie, are your parents' home?"

"They aren't, actually."

"When will they be home? You gave them the message that the dates of our business trip changed, didn't you?" asked Kimberly.

Charlie looked at Blair then flashed a smile. "Of course, I did. They just ran to the store and will be back shortly. Blair can run on up to Claire's room and they can play."

"Oh good, thank you, Charlie." Kimberly turned to her daughter. "Now you behave yourself for Charlie until the Robertson's get back. Have fun with Claire and maybe you girls can start planning what you want to do for your birthday. I love you."

"I love you, too, Mom, be safe."

Blair hugged her mom, ran inside and rushed up the stairs to her best friend's room. "Hey Claire, I'm…" Blair stopped when she noticed the room was empty.

Hearing a slight chuckle behind her, she turned around to see Charlie standing there with his hand over his mouth. "Where's Claire?"

"Yeah, about that. She's not here. Actually, no one is here but me. They had a family emergency and rushed away this morning."

"Oh, um, why didn't they tell my parents?" questioned Blair as she swirled a strand of hair around her finger. "Or why didn't you?"

"They said they would be back soon and to just keep an eye on you until they get back."

"Okay so why did you lie to my mom?" Blair pressed.

Charlie slapped her across the face. "Watch your tone, little girl. I didn't want to cause your mom to panic and mess up their trip, so I told a little white lie."

Blair cupped her cheek, still stinging from his slap and tightened the grip on her backpack. Something about him gave her an eerie feeling and she didn't like it at all. "Can I just hang here and wait for Claire to come home?"

"Of course, you can, Blairy," he said as he ruffled the top of her hair.

Once alone in her best friend's room, the eerie feeling faded away and the excitement returned. Throwing her bags on her favorite chair, she plopped down on the bed and pulled out her cell phone. She giggled to herself thinking about how mad her dad was when her mom got the cell phone for her. He felt she was too young to have one, but her mom who was over-protective, felt she needed it. She only used it to talk to them and talk to Claire.

Blair was typing a text to Claire when there was a slight knock on the door and Charlie walked in, carrying what looked like milk and cookies. Sitting her phone down before she sent the text, she took the milk and cookies from him.

"Thanks, Charlie, you didn't need to bring me this though."

"I just felt like I should because of what happened earlier. A sort of an apology, if you will. Besides, it would be a nice snack to help the time pass. I'll be downstairs in the living room if you need me," he said as he walked out of the room, closing the door behind him.

Shocked at his apology, she turned on the TV and ate her cookies and milk. It wasn't long after that she started to get sleepy and laid down letting the TV sounds drift her off into her dreams. Her dreams were wild, crazy, and felt very real. She felt as if she was moving even though she wasn't controlling her movements. A thunderous boom pulled her out of dreamland and back to reality. When Blair fully woke up, she was confused.

She was no longer in Claire's room on her bed. There was no TV, no milk and cookies on a tray. Looking around Blair had no idea where she was but felt as if she was in a small closet of some sort. She noticed a sleeping bag, pillow, blanket, and a few of Claire's books. There was a little glimmer coming from a tap light in the corner. She could tell the closet wasn't big enough for her to stand up fully, there were no windows, and only one door, that of course was locked.

Blair had never seen this closet before, and she knew every inch of her best friend's house. Was she even at her friend's still? Was this a crawl space in Charlie's room? Where were Claire and her parents? Blair started to freak out, banging and screaming on the door, but nothing happened. She began frantically crawling all around the closet on her knees looking for her phone. When she didn't find it, she curled up in the sleeping bag and rocked back and forth, crying silently.

****

Seven days; it had been seven days since Blair came over to her best friends. She kept track using a small crayon she found in the closet and made tally marks on the wall. She hadn't seen her best friend or anyone other than Charlie. The two best friends had so much planned and couldn't wait to spend several weeks together, but what was happening to Blair was not at all what they had planned. The last time she remembered being out of this closet was when she was having milk and cookies while watching TV in Claire's room. Charlie had put snacks in the closet, but it had to be when she was sleeping because she never heard or saw him.

Hearing the deadbolts unlock, Blair was snatched from her thoughts. Charlie reached in and pulled her out.

"She's right here," Charlie said as he handed Blair her phone.

Placing it up to her ear as she said "hello," only to quickly pull it back, not realizing it was on speaker.

"How are you sweetheart?" her mother asked cheerfully.

"I'm okay."

"Blair, what's wrong?" her mother questioned, noting the sadness in her daughter's voice. "Why did Charlie answer your phone?

Charlie flashed Blair a mean look, daring her to tell the truth.

"Nothing is wrong, Mom. I'm just waking up. He must have heard my phone ringing when I left it down in the kitchen." Blair lied.

"Oh, goodness, child. It's almost noon. Are you two girls going to sleep your time together away?"

"No, Mom. We stay up late at night."

"Ha, yes, that is true. I guess that's what preteens do these days, huh? Well, I just wanted to check on you and see how you were doing. We are about to go into a meeting. I will call you later. I love you, sweetie."

"I love you too, Mom."

The line went dead. Charlie snatched the phone from her hands and pushed her back into the closet. Blair listened as the four deadbolts locked and then the chain slid into place. She hung her head missing her parents more than ever. She wished she could have told her mom what was going on. Pulling her knees to her chest, she sat there on the middle of the sleeping bag trying not to cry; she didn't know how she was ever going to last another two weeks here.

She was mad that Claire and her parents weren't here yet; Charlie said they had a family emergency and would have been home soon, but where were they? She had only met Charlie a few times prior to this and he seemed fine then. He was about four years older than them, so they didn't hang around him much. Claire had always said he was the stepbrother from hell, but that was an understatement. He had to be the son of the devil himself.

Nobody was coming home; there was no point in trying to yell. However, Blair didn't stop looking for a way out. She knew this house like the back of her hand and if she could get out of this closet long enough, she could break free. He probably knew that too, which is why he didn't let her out of his sight for even a minute.

Blair heard the garage door open and held her breath while she listened for familiar voices, but there was none. She exhaled assuming it was Charlie leaving and began looking more frantically for a way out of this dreadful closet. Without any luck, she reluctantly gave up and lay down with her back toward the door. She was going to force herself back to sleep, thinking it would help ease her mind. Before Blair could even fall asleep, she heard the deadbolts and the door opened. Charlie reached in and pulled her out of the closet by her ponytail.

"Ouch, Charlie. That hurts," she yelled.

"I brought you lunch, brat so I would be nice to me. I didn't know what you'd like, but I figured you were hungry," he said as he pushed her toward the kitchen.

Blair was shocked; he hadn't let her eat a real meal since she's been here. She entered the kitchen where the smell of McDonald's made her mouth instantly water, stomach rumbling. For the last three days, she hadn't eaten even the snacks he would bring because he stopped bringing them. She quickly sat down staring at all the food in front of her; looking at him before she even took a bite.

"Go ahead girl, eat."

Blair grabbed a handful of fries and shoved them in her mouth, took a bite of hamburger and then a nugget, and washed it down with a big gulp of root beer. At this very moment, nothing else mattered; not even eating like a slob. She ate and ate until she couldn't eat anymore.

"Thank you for lunch, Charlie," Blair said as she got up and headed to the bathroom.

Charlie didn't say anything just followed her, standing outside the door. After she peed, she scooted past him, walking back to his room and headed to the closet. Before she could walk in fully inside the closet, Charlie pushed her causing her to bump her head on a nail that was slightly exposed. As a slight coolness ran down her forehead, the door slammed causing her to jump. Slumping down on the mattress, Blair wiped the blood from her head as tears ran down her face.

"Why did you push me?" she yelled through the door, tears streaming down her face.

"I don't know, maybe because I felt like it," Charlie said and locked the door.

Why was he doing this? Would Claire and her parents get home soon? Blair's mind raced as she got up and tried pushing on the door to get it open. Of course, she had no luck at all. Defeated, she curled up in a ball and cried herself to sleep hoping when she woke up everything would be back to normal.

Waking up a couple hours later, things weren't back to normal. Blair had a splitting headache for some reason. She rubbed her forehead and quickly remembered why her head hurt.

Charlie opened the door and stood there with a smile on his face. "Glad you're finally awake; you were out for a while."

"You pushed me, and I hit my head. What did you expect?" spat Blair.

"Ah, you have such a smart little mouth on you, Blair. I don't like smart-mouthed brats."

"Well, I don't like guys who keep young girls trapped in his closet!"

Charlie slapped her across the face causing her lip to bleed a little. "Listen, you little twat. I don't want to leave bruises, but I will if you make me."

"Why are you doing this?" Blair cried out.

"Mostly because I'm bored," answered Charlie nonchalantly.

"Seriously? You've got to be kidding me."

Charlie laughed so hard he had tears coming from his eyes and was almost rolling on the floor. Suddenly, the doorbell rang. Blair's eyes darted, looking around wondering if now was her best chance to run.

"Shit. I forgot they were coming," Charlie mumbled as the doorbell rang again and whoever was standing on the other side, began to knock. "All right all right, ya dick, I'm coming. Hold on," Charlie yelled.

Charlie left the room leaving Blair out of the closet for the first time ever. She stood still and waited to see what would happen next. Silence. Nothing happened; he must have left. She quickly got up and said aloud to herself, “I’ve got to get out of here.”

Dashing like the speed of light, she made her way to the front door, but came to a quick halt when she heard keys in the door. Fearing it was Charlie, she turned and ran through the kitchen to the back door as fast as she could. She flung the door open and ran…

Right into Charlie.

“And where do you think you are going, my sweets?”

“I feel like I’m going to hell.”

“Chin up buttercup, hell isn’t as bad as you think,” Charlie sang with laughter.

Not even reaching for a knife to cut him, or the vase on the table to harm him, Blair despondly moved as Charlie pulled her back through the kitchen by her hair. Her eyes were on the floor, head hung low. She didn’t need to look, she knew he was taking her back to his closet. Her eyes stayed on the floor until they stopped walking and she saw a pair of shoes. Following them up the legs and to the face, her heart began pounding. Charlie’s grip on her hair loosened and Blair ran straight into the arms of her best friend's mom.

“What in the heavens is going on?” she questioned frantically as she looked over Blair. “What happened to her face, Charlie?”

“Oh, I was just having some fun with Blair,” Charlie shrugged.

“Charlie get your ass over here,” demanded his dad fists balled tightly.

“Blair, honey, come tell me what happened,” her friend’s mom said with calmness in her voice.

Blair looked to Claire who reached out for her hand and squeezed it tight. Taking a deep breath, Blair let it all out, tears included. She shared every single detail; from the time she got here until now. The entire time she could feel Charlie watching her, a smile on his face.

“Kevin, this is unacceptable,” Claire's mom said to her husband.

“I know, Danielle. Go call the cops.” Kevin turned to Blair. “Sweetheart, I am so sorry my son did this to you. His actions will not go unpunished. I know that won't take away what he did, but I hope that will ease your mind because he will never hurt you again."

Claire took Blair to her room to wait for the police while her mom called Blair's parents; they were taking the next flight out.

"Blair, I am so sorry my step brother did this to you."

"Claire, I was so scared. I was so mad. I knew you said he was evil, but I couldn't even imagine he was doing this just because he was bored. Like who keeps a girl locked in their closet for fun?"

"I kept telling my mom and Kevin over and over he was mean to me. They didn't believe me at all. They thought I was just being a little brat who was jealous of my mom's new boyfriend and son. I understand if you don't want to be my friend anymore."

"Claire, it wasn't your fault. He's a very sick guy; he needs help," Blair stated, not mentioning that she too, would need help.

CHAPTER TWO

Eleven years and a few therapists later, Blair decided it was time to get out of her parent's house. She was twenty-three years old but didn't feel like a real adult. Since the incident that happened when she was younger, she hardly left home; she was too afraid of getting taken again. She even finished out the rest of her schooling online. Her parents felt so bad about what had happened with Charlie, they didn't force her to do anything and that included moving out. Hating that they blamed themselves, she wanted them to know that she would make it in the real world, and on her own eventually.

She was browsing online one rainy afternoon looking for apartments when she came across the perfect listing. The price wasn't posted, but everything else was very appealing. It was a single level house that had the perfect set up; a couple of bedrooms, privacy fence, and the garage attached. She read it had a top of the line security system installed, with motion sensor lights, and cameras all around. Convinced it was just for her, she talked her dad into going to look at it with her.

When they pulled up her dad, Tony, was impressed at how nice the house looked, but he noticed there was no for rent or sale sign in the yard. Unsure about this, he got out of the car and followed his daughter to the front door. She knocked and they waited and waited, but nobody came. He looked in through the window and saw that the house was completely empty before he could say anything, the front door opened. A tall, slender man in his late thirties appeared.

"Sorry about that. I was in the garage," he said, giving Blair a quick smile. "I'm Nathan. How can I help you guys?"

"I'm Tony. My daughter, Blair, saw the listing for your house online and just had to come check it out. But I didn't see a for sale sign, have you already sold?" he questioned.

"I haven't sold yet. It's just been on the market for so many months I took the sign down," Nathan lied. "It was my brother's house and he had specific instructions on who should be able to have his house, so I have to be very selective on the new owner. If you would like, I can show you guys around."

"I would love that," Blair squealed.

Nathan smiled and took them on a tour of the house. He and his brother hadn't always gotten along that's why he wanted to honor his dying wishes for his house. He promised Chadwick that he would only show the house to the girl he named and that he wouldn't tell her more than what he wanted her to know. His brother was a computer nut that had impressed him all his life. Even after his death, he was still impressing him. Unsure how Chadwick knew this girl's name to put in his will, Nathan kept his curiosity to himself and continued showing them around.

"So, what did you think?" Nathan asked when they made it back to the front door

"It's so beautiful. I love that he had a top of the line security system. I've never seen one like it before. I love the…"

"That's enough Blair," Tony said, cutting her off. "Sorry, my daughter has an obsession with technology."

"That's perfectly fine," Nathan chucked. "My brother did too. As a matter of fact, he created and built his own security system and the features in the house."

Blair's mouth dropped. "No way? That is phenomenal!!"

"Now honey, don't get too excited. I'm sure this house is way out of our price range."

"But dad…"

"Yes, I know you are grown, have a good job, and some money saved up, but I don't know if buying this expensive of a house would be a smart decision."

"We don't even know how much it is," protested Blair.

"Probably too…"

"Can I cut in?" interrupted Nathan. "Actually, the house is paid for and my brother didn't want anything for it. You would just have to pay property tax. He just wanted to make sure the new owner took care of it and the security system. He loved this house so much, it was his pride and joy."

"Wait, I don't understand. You're just supposed to give the house away to some stranger and not take a dime for it?" questioned Tony confused.

"That's correct. My brother and I didn't always get along, but when he became ill with cancer, I tried to make right by him. This was his last dying wish and I promised him I would honor it. I have no ill intentions either. He made up a contract before he died that I had to sign proving so. He also made a contract for the house's new owner. You guys can look at all of that first and then it could be yours. I am only supposed to be here to help find the house a great new owner. And maybe help with maintenance if needed."

"If you've shown it to other people, how come you didn't give it to any of them? Why me?" inquired Blair.

"As I've mentioned, my brother had a strict set of rules for me when picking the new owner. You are the first person to appreciate his security system. Everyone else wanted to get rid of it one way or another. And that was most definitely a no for my brother; security system had to stay just how it was."

Tony looked over both the contracts twice before he felt like Nathan was being true to his word. He couldn't find anything in small print or hidden that would affect his daughter if she were to take ownership of the house. He listened as Nathan talked about his brother and felt like he was really trying to honor his brother's dying wish. Giving Blair the okay to make the final decision, he knew she would walk away happier than ever as a new homeowner.

Nathan couldn't help but feel at peace when Blair signed the contract. She was in her early to mid-twenties. He couldn't tell for sure. Her appreciation for the security system proved she wasn't your typical young woman. Unsure how his brother knew this girl would become the owner of his house was beyond him. Once they finished up, Nathan watched them drive away knowing that one day, he may have a lot of questions to answer and he wasn't sure if he was quite ready for that.

CHAPTER THREE

Two months after Blair found her house, she had officially moved in. Her parents felt as if she wasn't ready to be on her own yet and did everything to talk her out of moving. To be honest, she wasn't sure if she would be able to do it either, but she was done letting fear control her life. Her therapist agreed with the move but made her promise to move back to her parents if it became too much. Besides, Blair felt as if the house was made just for her. The security system really made her feel safe.

She blindfolded herself and made sure she could navigate throughout her house without sight. Hidden strategically all over the house were objects that could be used as a weapon should someone get inside. Blair was positive that if someone broke in, she would be able to defend herself with little to no harm done to her; she felt safer then she had in years.

Since she had been doing so well with the move, her therapist had been trying to convince her to get out of the house and out on the town. For months Blair wouldn't even try. For some reason today, Blair felt like going to the market in town. Once she stepped onto the crowded, Saturday afternoon streets, she regretted it completely. There were more people out then she expected. Trying to calm her breathing in hopes she wouldn't have a panic attack, Blair just stood right there in the middle of everyone not moving a muscle; mind in another place.

Trey was sitting at the park with his cousins and little sister when he saw her. She had long black hair that came down past the middle of her back and was standing in the middle of the crowded sidewalk with panic written all over her face. Trey scanned the crowd trying to see what could have spooked the girl, but he saw nothing out of the ordinary. Out of nowhere comes a man who puts something over her head and throws her into a nearby van. After he jumped in, the van sped off.

Trey yelled at his cousin to watch his sister then ran to his car. He caught up to the van and grabbed his phone to call 911, but forgot his phone died over an hour ago. Not knowing what else to do, he plugged his phone into his car charger and kept following. The van took him from the middle of town, to the outside of town, and now they were on some country road he had never been on before. Trey was unsure of where they were possibly going, but he didn't turn back. He had to help this girl.

Finally, after following the van outside of town for fifteen minutes, the van pulled into a driveway. Trey drove past the driveway a few feet then shut off his car. He grabbed his phone, that charged almost halfway, locked his car, and walked back to the driveway. From his spot behind the bushes, he saw the van pull up to the house. Five men jumped out and two pushed the girl inside. Feeling a little outnumbered with only his phone and a pocket knife, Trey crept closer to the house trying to stay out of sight questioning why he didn't just call the cops and not be a hero tonight.

Back inside the house, a man pushed Blair down into a chair. He tied her up before he removed the cover from her head.

"Shocked to see me, baby girl?"

"Charlie? When did you get out of jail? How did you find me?"

"Who said I ever lost you, Blair?" laughed Charlie along with the other guys.

"What do you want?"

"Don't act like you don't know. You put me away for having a little fun and it broke my heart and pissed me off," Charlie said with an evil smile.

"One must have a heart before it could be broken," mumbled Blair.

"There's that smart mouth that got you in trouble as a kid. You would think you would've learned by now."

"After being locked up for several years, you think you would have learned too, Charlie," Blair raised her eyebrows, smile outlined her face.

Charlie didn't like what he heard. He reared back and slapped her right across the face, causing an instant handprint to form. He didn't just stop after that slap, he kept going until his hands were covered in blood. Blair begged him to stop between each hit, but it was like he didn't hear her. Right as he was about to punch her in the stomach, his phone rang.

"We gotta go, boys. Be good, my precious Blair. I will be back for you," Charlie called as he walked out of the door.

Trey, who had watched the whole thing helplessly, moved to the other side of the house. He watched until the van's tail lights were out of sight before he tried the door. Locked. He made his way back to the side of the house and tried a window. The house was old and rundown, but the window slid up with just a few creeks. Trey jumped inside causing Blair to jerk back, scared.

"Who are you?" asked Blair.

Trey jumped a little not expecting her to have seen him. "I'm just an innocent bystander, here to save you."

"Bystander? You mean you aren't one of Charlie's boys sent here to watch me?"

"I don't know who Charlie is, but I've gathered he's the one callin' the shots. He was the one who hit you right?"

Blair nodded.

"I ain't one of his boys, but I am here to help. I was in the park when I saw you and thought you were very beautiful, the fear that was written all over your face is why I couldn't look away. Then I saw them grab you and throw you in the van. I would have just called 911, but my damn phone was dead, so I followed. Now, let's get out of here before they come back. I'm sort of outnumbered here."

Trey untied Blair and helped her out of the window not bothering to close it as they left. He led the way back to his car where she was close behind. Once inside the car he quickly drove off, not waiting on her to buckle up.

"I'm Blair, by the way. And thank you for saving me," she pushed a smile on her swollen face.

"I'm Trey. My mamma did raise me right. I couldn't just leave you once I saw them take you. Who are those guys anyway?"

"It's a long story."

"We have a fifteen-minute drive back to town."

"Good point, but no offense, but I don't know you. I don't feel comfortable sharing my story with a stranger. I will say this though, for eleven years I haven't seen or heard from him and I have no idea how he found me," shared Blair.

"Oh, nah, girl, no offence taken. I understand. That's fucked up though; what he did to you. I should take you to the hospital to have you checked out."

"No, no I'm fine. Can you just please take me home?"

Agreeing reluctantly, the rest of the ride Trey tried making small talk to take her mind off what just happened. He offered to take her to the hospital again, but she politely declined. Against his better judgment, he did what she asked and took her home. Once in Blair's driveway, he stalled.

"Are you sure I can't take you to the hospital? I don't mind."

"You've done enough already. I'm fine, really."

"Do you need me to go in with you and check around your place to make sure nobody is in there?"

Blair chuckled a little. "Oh no, nobody is in there. I've got a great security system. But how can I ever repay you?"

"You could go to dinner with your hero in a week or two just so I know you're seriously okay."

"Trey, you seem like a nice guy, but I'm not looking to date anyone," Blair stated bluntly.

"A date?" guffawed Trey. "Who said it would be a date? Think of it more like the hero checkin' in," he threw out trying to regain himself.

"If I gave you my number, would you please stop begging me?" teased Blair with a smile.

"I can't make any promises, but I'll work on it."

Blair laughed and gave Trey her number and thanked him again. She walked inside her house, turning off and on her alarm, watching him pull out of her driveway. After he left, she went to wipe her face and ice it, making a mental note not to tell her mom about what happened.

Today was way too weird for her to comprehend. The fact that Charlie found her scared her more than she wanted to admit, but Trey coming to her rescue restored some of her faith in humanity. She wanted to think all people were bad because of Charlie, but that wasn't fair to anyone else. Maybe it was time to make some ample changes to her life and leave her house more often.

****

Trey laid in bed thinking about the day he just had. He couldn't believe it all happened the way it did. He wouldn't consider himself the hero type usually, but today he couldn't help himself. They were lucky it was so easy to get Blair out of there before those guys came back. He still wished he could have taken her to the hospital though. There was something about Blair that made him want to get to know her story.

Glancing at the clock on his nightstand, it read 2:30 in the morning. Trey rolled over and forced his mind to think about things that bore him. Right as he was falling asleep, screams woke him up, causing him to jump out of bed. He ran right to his sister's room and tried to comfort her until she would wake up.

"Ebaleah, wake up sweetie. It's only a dream," Trey said in a calm voice.

Ebaleah woke up and looked around her room. When she realized she was safe, she buried her face in her brother's chest. "I'm sorry Trey. I didn't mean to wake you."

"It's okay Eb. When did the nightmares start again?"

"Honestly, they never stopped. Will they ever stop, Trey?"

"I don't know, Sis, I really don't. Why didn't you tell me they hadn't stopped? Do you want to start seeing your therapist again?"

Ebaleah waited for a moment before she responded. "I wanted to try and get them under control myself before we go back there."

"That sounds like a good plan. Anything I can do to help?"

"Just lay with me until I fall asleep."

Trey agreed and they laid next to each other not saying another word. Trey's heart ached for his baby sister. At thirteen years old she has seen more than any thirteen-year-old should. He tried to protect her from any and everything since that dark night three years ago. Trey drifted off to sleep with his sister in his arms fast asleep.

Trey woke the next morning to the smell of food, he rubbed his eyes and got out of his sister's bed. Eyes half open, he made his way to the kitchen, his nose leading the way. Trey stood in the kitchen rubbing his eyes again to make sure he wasn't seeing things. Ebaleah turned around and laughed.

"Good morning, sleepy head. About time you wake up."

"I had too. I didn't want my sister burning down our apartment," teased Trey as he sat at the table.

"Hey!" she said with a playful push to his chest. "I'm a pretty good cook."

"We'll see about that. Got to make sure I don't die after eating your food."

"Oh, stop it, Trey. You've had my cooking before and you are still here!"

"You are right. It's gonna take more than some bad cooking to get rid of me."

"Oh brother." Ebaleah rolled her eyes. "Sit yo tail there and be quiet. It's almost ready then I'll make your plate."

"Why you doin' this today, Sis?" questioned Trey.

"What? I can't do something nice for my brother?"

"You can, but you usually want something," he stated with a raised eyebrow.

"I just want to thank you, Trey. You do so much for me. And honestly, I don't think I could have gone back to sleep last night if it wasn't for you. I know you can't sleep with me every night, but I'm glad you did. I know you are right up the hall if anything were to happen, you would be there in a heartbeat. I couldn't ask for a better big brother," Ebaleah admitted, kissing Trey on the cheek.

Trey had a lump in his throat. His sister always knew how to choke him up. Clearing his throat, he said, "That's what big brothers are for, Eb. You haven't had it easy and I'd do anything I could to take away that pain. It's not ideal for big brothers to sleep with their little sisters, but if you need me to sleep in your room sometimes, I can sleep on the floor."

"I appreciate that, bub. I really do. I am kinda too old for teddy bears and cuddles with my big brother," Ebaleah hung her head. "I'll figure something out."

"Hey, Sis, you ain't in this alone," Trey said, lifting her head. "What if we got a dog?"

"A dog? Are you serious right now?"

"I am so serious right now," Trey said in a girly voice. "We could even make it a service dog if you needed it to go with you places like school or whatever."

Ebaleah jumped up and down, letting out a slight squeal. She ran and hugged her brother so tight he thought he was going to pass out. Smiling at his sister's excitement, he knew he had made the right choice. Besides, they could train the dog to be protective as well so he wouldn't be worried when Eb wasn't by his side. This gave him a great idea. He went to his room, grabbed his phone and made a quick phone call.

"Hey Trey," Blair said upon answering.

"How's it goin', Blair?"

"Pretty good over here. Please don't tell me you called to ask me on a date," Blair joked.

"As much as I know you would just love to go on a date with me, that isn't exactly why I called. How do you feel about dogs?"

"Um, they are okay, I guess. I've never actually had a dog. Why are you asking about dogs?" Blair asked.

"My sister and I were talking about gettin' a dog and I thought that maybe having a dog could help you, too."

"Help me how?"

"I don't mean to overstep here or anything, but you hardly leave your house. You have a security system that probably costs more than I've made as long as I've been living, and you seem like you could use an excuse to get out of the house."

"Ah, I dunno, Trey. A dog seems like a lot of work and between working and my training, I dunno if I'll have the time for one."

"Your training? You work too?"

"Yes, I work from home. When I'm not working, I'm doing self-defense training."

"Man, that dude really messed you up, huh?"

"Excuse me?"

"Look, Blair. I'm sorry. I didn't mean to upset you. I don't know the whole situation and I'm clearly no expert, but I think shutting yourself off from the world is a terrible idea. You can train and prepare your whole life, but you will never be fully prepared for everything. Stop letting him control your entire life."

"You don't know me or what happened. Besides what do you know about any of this?" spat Blair defensively.

"You are right. I don't know you or what happened. I would love to get to know you though, Blair. You are a beautiful young lady. From what I've learned so far, you seem pretty smart and sort of witty; qualities I just happen to enjoy. I'll tell you this. I may not know anything about what you're dealing with, but I know how traumatic situations can turn your entire world upside down especially if you experience them at a young age. I know how those situations don't just affect you, but everyone around you."

"I know just because that situation happened years ago, it doesn't go away. You relive it over and over each and every day. I know what it's like to feel helpless and have no control. I also know how it feels to be completely alone. I don't know your story

Blair, but if you ever want to share, I'll be ready to listen. Even if you don't think having a dog would do you any good at all, would you consider going with me and my sister to help us pick out a dog for her?"

Blair sat there in her bedroom, speechless. She clearly didn't know what Trey was going through, though he spoke with such passion and pain. She felt sort of selfish and like she was being childish. He saved her before so she would be safe with him, wouldn't she? Before her heart could begin to process everything, her mouth began to move.

"I would love to go with you guys."

"Whew, I was worried my lil' rant scared you off."

"Honestly, it was unexpected, but you are so right. I need to take control of my life again. I just needed the right person to push me to do it. Now, when are we going to look at dogs?"

Trey told her his schedule for the week, and they worked out a day that would work best for the both. By the time they got off the phone, Blair was more excited then she thought she would be. Before she could put her phone down, it rang again. It was her mom.

"Hey, Mom. How are you?"

"I'm good honey. How are you?"

"Honestly Mom, I'm great. I've been thinking, you should really let me install a security system at your house. I want you and dad to stay safe."

"Oh Blair, we don't know anything about that kind of stuff. Your father would probably set it off more than anyone," Blair's mom chuckled.

Blair laughed, too. "I could show you both how to work it. I would make sure it's as easy as 1-2-3 for you guys. Please try to talk him into it, Mom. For me."

"Okay honey, I'll try. Just for you."

"Thanks, Mom. Oh, I may be getting a dog."

"A dog? What in the heavens for?"

"Trey, a new friend of mine, he suggested it. He also suggested I stop letting my past control so much of my future. Having a dog around me may help."

"Now who does this guy think he is? Doesn't he know what Charlie did to you? Doesn't he know all that you've done to keep yourself safe?"

"Mom, he's just trying to be a friend. He knows a little bit about Charlie and about how I protect myself. He also knows I don't have control over my life. By staying in the house all the time, that is giving Charlie the control."

"He is no therapist, Blair," her mother stated harshly.

"You're right, he's not. But he's right. My actual therapist has said the same things. I just took them differently."

"Why the sudden change now?"

"Mom, I'm twenty-three years old. I work from home and hardly leave my house. I have no friends. Nobody except you and dad come to visit. I'm still a virgin. I literally have no real life. I am still living the life of the victim. I need to stop thinking that everyone is like Charlie and out to get me. Besides, I'm not too sure, but I think Trey's little sister may have gone through something life changing too and she's not locking herself in her house alone."

"Okay, okay you've convinced me. Just promise me you'll be careful."

"I promise. I love you, Mom."

"I love you, too, sweetheart."

CHAPTER FOUR

"Now, Ebaleah, I want you to be on your best behavior today. One of my new friends is gonna join us and I don't want you to upset her," Trey warned on the drive to Blair's.

"Trey, do you have a crush?"

"No, Sis. She's just a friend."

"Then why are you so worried about how I act?"

"Remember that day we were in the park and I ran off? I ran off to save her and apparently, she's had some rough things happen to her that's caused her to shut out the world and never leave her house."

"What kind of rough things? How did you save her that day if she never leaves her house? How did you get her to come with us if she never leaves her house?" rambled Ebaleah.

"Enough with the questions, Sis. I'm sure if things go okay today, you guys can both share your stories one day."

"My story? Like what ...what I saw that night?"

Trey placed a hand on his sister's knee. "Yes, like what you saw that night. I know it may be hard at first, but maybe it could help Blair. Who knows, maybe you can help people all over if you ever decide to share your story. Now, hop out and get in the backseat," Trey said as he jumped out, heading up to Blair's house.

He knocked and waited for her to come out. Once she opened the door, she stopped to set the alarm, then followed him to the car. He opened the car door for her then slid back into the driver seat. After a quick introduction, he drove them to the nearest humane society.

"I've been doing a lot of research on training dogs or making them service dogs. It looks rather expensive so I thought we should start here first. Any dog could be trained, and these dogs need homes."

Blair smiled. She couldn't believe he did research on this stuff. His sister was obviously important to him. "It sounds like a win-win to me!"

They headed inside and were greeted by a lady sitting behind a counter whose name tag read Sally. "Welcome guys. What can we help you with today?"

"Well, my sister and I are looking to get a dog. Preferably one that could be trained with certain commands."

"You came to the right place. Most of the dogs here are very trainable. Our staff works with them daily and we put them through several tests. Would you like a medium sized dog or one smaller? What type of commands would you like it to learn?"

"A medium-sized dog would be good. I haven't thought too much into it, but I would like it to be able to protect my sister."

Sally smiled and walked from behind the counter. "Most dogs have an instinct to protect when they sense their owner in danger. The same goes if they sense their owner is sad; dogs have amazing senses. We can give you a list of some dog trainers in the area that can help perfect any training you want."

Sally lead them to a glass door. Through that door, you could see rows and rows of cages filled with different dogs and cats. "There are a lot of dogs waiting to be adopted. Why don't you guys go ahead and start looking around? When you find one you like, come find me or any staff member, and we can take them out for you and let you get acquainted with them."

"Thank you so much," Trey said as he led the way inside.

Ebaleah squealed with excitement rushing past her brother to the first cage. They went cage by cage looking at all the different dogs, some of which were still puppies. Blair tried not to really look at them, but she grew attached to this female Pitbull named Jazmine. Her steel grey coat with those big baby blue eyes tugged at Blair's heart. She was so busy petting Jazmine through the cage that she hadn't noticed Trey and Ebaleah weren't around.

"Thought you didn't want a dog," teased Trey as he walked up behind her.

"I honestly didn't. Then I saw Jazmine and my feelings changed. I think I want to take her out. Has Ebaleah found a dog she likes?"

"She found about ten."

They both laughed. "She found a pity named Ace that she absolutely adores. She is outside with him now. Would you like to take Jazmine out? I can go grab someone for you."

"Yeah, that would be awesome. Thank you."

After two hours, they were heading to the pet store with their new dogs, Jazmine, and Ace, who got along perfectly. Ebaleah suggested getting food, toys, and treats for them since the humane society gave them a collar and leash. The day seemed to be going so well that after the store Blair suggested they go back to her house to let the dogs play since she had a huge backyard. Ebaleah loved the idea! Trey liked it as well considering it gave him more time to get to know Blair who secretly enjoyed their company.

Trey went inside to use the bathroom, leaving Blair and Ebaleah to talk.

"I'm glad you caved and got Jazmine. I think she could really help you," admitted Ebaleah.

"Help me?" questioned Blaire confused.

"Trey told me about you hardly leaving your house. Maybe having Jazmine will change that for you."

"Eb!" Trey yelled walking back outside, embarrassed.

Blair smiled. "It's okay, Trey. You are right, though, Ebaleah. Hopefully having Jazmine will help me get out of the house more. I hope Ace will help you, too. I'm glad you guys invited me."

"We're glad you came," Ebaleah chirped.

****

Blair started working with Jazmine teaching her simple commands and she seemed to be picking up quickly; Blair was rather impressed. Giving Jasmine some treats, she sat on the couch and watched her play with her new toys. There was a knock at the door. Jazmine dropped her toy and stood up, looking right at the door. Blair walked to the door, clicking on the camera pad to see who was knocking.

Blair's jaw dropped when she saw Charlie standing there. How did he find her house? What did he want? Not knowing what to do, she just stood there not moving. Jazmine was right by her side, ears up alert. Charlie reaches up and pushed the button to speak.

"Blair, are you home?"

"Blair, if you're in there, just know I do know where you live. I will be back. I want to talk to you," Charlie said when she didn't say anything.

Blair watched as he walked back to his car and drove away. She pressed her back against the door and slid down to the floor. She tried hard to fight it, but the tears came; slowly at first. She finally just let it out. She cried and cried. Some of the tears were because of fear, but most of them were from anger. She was so angry she let him scare her this much and control her life.

Jazmine was right there licking the tears off her face. Blair smiled and wrapped her arm around her sweet dog's body. Jazmine leaned on Blair's shoulder, nuzzling her neck and face. Slowly, Blair stopped crying. She pulled herself up off the ground, checking the camera before she walked back into the living room and Jazmine back to her toys.

Blair's phone rang, causing her to jump.

"Hey, Trey."

"Hey, Blair. How are you?"

"I'm okay. How are you?"

"I'm fine. Blair, are you sure you're okay? Sounds like something is wrong."

Blair was quiet for a moment before she told him about her recent visitor.

"Did he leave? Are you okay, seriously?"

"He left. To be honest, I … I really don't know."

"Hang tight. I'm on my way over."

CHAPTER FIVE

It was ten pm before Blair realized how late it had gotten. They had been talking for hours, sitting close on the couch. "Trey it's late. Don't you need to get home to your sister?"

"I don't. She's staying the night at a friend's. But I can leave if you want me too."

"Oh no, you're fine. I'm enjoying your company. I just didn't want to keep you away from her real late."

"Thank you for thinking about that. Did Charlie say when he was coming back?" Trey asked nervously.

"He didn't. I don't know why he was here in the first place. Or how he even found my house."

"Do you think you would be comfortable going to the cops?"

"Will it do any good?"

"Tell you what, if you don't mind, I'll ask a buddy of my cousins to see what he suggests. He's a cop."

"I guess that couldn't hurt."

Trey promised to talk to him soon and let her know. He then turned their attention to Jazmine. He noticed how she hadn't left Blair's side since he arrived two hours ago.

"She's such a sweetheart. I'm really glad I went with you guys and got her."

"I'm glad too. If you're up for it, we should take the dogs to the park someday."

"I don't want to say no, but I can't say yes either. Not yet."

"It's fine, I understand. I couldn't get Ebaleah out of her room for weeks. When I finally was able to get her out of the room, getting her to leave the house was another issue. She was falling so far behind in school and I was too. I couldn't get to her no matter what. Then one day it was like a flip was switched and she was back to her old self; for the most part. I don't know exactly what happened, but I'm so glad to have my sister back even though things aren't perfect now. Sorry for rambling," Trey blushed when he realized he had been going on and on about his sister.

"I don't mind at all. I like listening to you talk. Besides, I can tell you really care about your sister."

"We are all we've got."

"I'm glad you have each other."

Soon as Blair stopped talking, Trey's lips were pressing against hers. She was completely shocked but didn't push him away; didn't make him stop. Blair surprised herself by kissing him back, starting to enjoy it. Before she could do anything else, Trey pulled away, his face flushed.

"I'm...I'm so sorry, Blair," Trey stuttered as he jumped up, running for the door.

Blair jumped up and ran after him. She grabbed his arm right as his hand gripped the doorknob.

"Trey, don't leave, please."

"I... I can't stay, Blair. I shouldn't have done that," he said, unable to make eye contact.

Blair grabbed his face and made him look at her. "You didn't do anything wrong. It was just a kiss. A nice kiss, but a kiss nonetheless."

"I'm really into you Blair. Have been from the first time I met you. And I know you don't want anything right now, but you were sitting so close and I couldn't stop thinking about how I really wanted to kiss you. I have terrible timing."

"Don't beat yourself up. You did nothing wrong, Trey. I said I would never leave my house. I did and I met you. I never wanted a dog until I met you. You talked me into leaving my house to go to look at dogs and I had a blast! I now have a great dog and two new friends. I'm not the same woman I was before I met you, Trey. I'm changing. I feel safe with you and you make me comfortable. So, if you want to leave, please only leave because of that and not because you kissed me."

"My life has changed since I met you, too, Blair. I've been so devoted to taking care of my sister that I forget I have wants and needs too. I haven't been interested in anyone in so long, but

I am so very, very interested in you. I respect you way too much to stay because that kiss made me feel things I haven't felt in years."

"I respect that. And I respect you, too. Will I talk to you tomorrow?"

"You will, Blair, I promise. Good night."

Trey leaned down and kissed Blair on the forehead then headed to his car. Blair closed the door and reset the alarm. She turned around smiling and saw Jazmine sitting there, tail wagging with a smile on her face too.

"I think I may like him girl," Blair said to Jazmine as she patted her head.

Walking into her room, Jazmine jumped on Blair's bed and walked in a circle before she laid down. Blair took off her clothes tossing them into the dirty hamper. She grabbed an oversized t-shirt from her dresser and put it on before climbing in bed next to Jazmine. She was about to close her eyes when she got a text from Trey saying he made it home and goodnight. She couldn't stop smiling. Wishing she had a girlfriend to talk too, she rolled over, plugged in her phone, then closed her eyes thinking that would be her next thing to tackle.

****

Trey laid in bed staring at the ceiling, unable to sleep. Even though he was still embarrassed, he was glad Blair didn't freak out on him. He felt giddy like a schoolgirl with a crush. He couldn't wait until Ebaleah came home tomorrow so he could tell her. She is going to eat this up and never let him live it down. He laughed out loud thinking about it before his phone rang interrupting his thoughts. It was his sister.

"Eb, what's wrong?" Trey asked, sitting up in bed.

"Trey, it's Melanie, Samantha's mom. Ebaleah is having an episode and it's bad."

"I'm on my way."

Throwing on his shoes and grabbing the keys he ran out of his room. Once at Samantha's house, he was met by Melanie who was standing on the porch. He followed her to the bathroom where she stood aside and motioned for him to go on in. He saw his sister in the small space between the toilet and the bathroom sink. She didn't look at him, but past him as if she was in another dimension. After ten minutes, Trey was able to get her back to reality and out of the bathroom.

"What happened?" Trey asked Melanie.

"Well, the girls wanted to watch a scary movie, and Samantha's brother decided to play a prank on them."

"And this was okay? Didn't you remember from the last time that scary movies are a no for Ebaleah?"

"I didn't think it would be an issue. She seemed fine all day and the girls really wanted to watch it. They were getting tired of watching chick flicks. I mean it's a sleepover. That's what they do."

"I'm sure Samantha has sleepovers all the time that Ebaleah doesn't attend. During those, it is perfectly fine to do whatever scary thing they want to do. But the one time she IS here, I expect you, as the adult and mother, to respect my simple request to not have scary movies played. But that is fine. You won't have to worry about her being an inconvenience at any other sleepovers."

Trey stormed off carrying his sister to the car. He was furious that this happened. He couldn't understand how anyone didn't understand the seriousness of Ebaleah's condition. Unable to shake his anger, he took his sister home and got her ready for bed. Ace was right by her side soon as she walked in the door. He could sense something was wrong and Trey loved that. Tucking his sister into bed, he kissed her forehead and watched as Ace laid down with his head on her shoulder.

As Trey walked back to his room, he realized he was shaking. He needed to calm down. He sat on his bed and took a couple of deep breaths. That didn't help. He went to the bathroom and splashed water on his face. That still didn't help. He picked up his phone and dialed Blair's number.

"Shit," he said aloud when he realized what time it was.

"Trey?" said Blair in a sleepy voice.

"Blair, I didn't think you would pick up."

"I'm a light sleeper. Trey, what's wrong?"

"Ebaleah's friend's and their stupid parents. They don't take her condition serious. Scary movies really do a number on her so it's one of my requests for them to not be played while she is staying over. Not only did the girls watch a scary movie tonight, the brother of the girl who had the sleepover scared them. Eb was so terrified it was like she was in a new dimension or something. I haven't seen her so tapped out of reality in so long. And the mother acted like it was no big deal."

"Are you serious? That is complete bullshit. I'm so sorry. How is she …."

Before Blair could finish, Ebaleah started screaming.

"I'm sorry Blair, I've got to go. I'll call you back."

Dropping his phone, Trey ran to his sister's room jumping in her bed and grabbing her. He held her and rocked her back and forth while he reassured her that it was just a dream. Finally, she woke up.

"Trey...I'm so sorry."

"Don't you dare. Hush Eb, you're fine."

"I never should have gone to that stupid sleepover. I don't like them girls anyway."

"Good cause you ain't going back over there. That insensitive bitch."

"Trey!"

"I'm sorry, but she pissed me off acting like it wasn't a big deal. That is not…."

There was a knock at the door.

"Trey, who is that?"

"I don't know. Stay here. Ace, don't leave her side, boy."

Ace stood up next to Ebaleah while Trey walked to the door, looked out the window, and saw Blair's car.

"Blair, what are you doing here?" he asked upon opening the door.

"I'm sorry I didn't wait for your call. You seemed really upset and I wanted to help. So, I just drove over before I had too much time to talk myself out of it."

"Well get in here then, it's chilly out."

Blair walked in and sat her purse down on the floor.

"Trey? Trey who's there?" Ebaleah asked from the hallway.

"It's just Blair. I was on the phone with her when you started screaming. She rushed over because she wanted to help."

"Aw Blair, that is really sweet. Usually, I would say something like 'you didn't have to come all this way' or 'I'll be fine' but I'm glad you came. To be honest, I don't want to go to sleep. I'm so scared of what tricks my mind will play on me."

"Well, it is a Friday night. Or I guess more of an early Saturday morning, but it's the weekend so we can stay up all night if you need to okay?"

"Thanks, Blair. Can you guys come to my room with me?"

"Of course, sis. We'll be right there."

Trey grabbed Blair and pulled her close to him. His hand rested behind her ear as he pulled her face to his for a kiss that held so much emotion, he was sure Ace could feel it down the hall.

"It means a lot to me that you risked your own fear to come to check on us," his voice cracked.

"Honestly, I wasn't thinking about me at all. All I could think about were the two of you and the next thing I knew I was knocking on your door."

Unable to say anything else with the fear he may shed a tear, Trey led her to Ebaleah's room. They sat on her bed and talked for hours. They laughed and laughed helping Ebaleah forget she was scared. They each shared stories, getting to know each other more. Finally, Ebaleah started to get tired. She wanted Blair to sleep with her and of course Blair didn't object. As happy as Trey was that his sister felt comfortable enough with Blair, he felt slightly jealous for more than one reason. Taking his jealous butt to bed he passed out soon as his head hit the pillow.

The next morning Trey woke to the sound of laughter coming from his sister's room. Smiling, he laid there listening; he loved the sound of his sister's laugh. In the thirteen years she had been alive, she'd been through way more than enough, yet she still amazed him every day. Blair amazed him last night as well. He knew it was hard for her to leave her house, especially at night, but she did it. Maybe having them in her life was helping her more than they all knew. He jumped up and headed for the shower.

Back in Ebaleah's room, she felt like opening up some. There was something about Blair that made her feel safe. Maybe her brother was right. Maybe if she shared her story, she could help someone. Ebaleah had never told anyone, other than her brother, about what she witnessed that night many years ago. She tried, without luck, to forget it. Maybe now was the time to take control. What if keeping it to herself was the reason behind all the nightmares? What if talking about it would finally make her feel in control again? But what if talking about it made things worse? Unable to decide which would be best, Ebaleah took a chance.

"Blair, can I ask you something?"

"Yeah, sure. Ask me anything."

"Were you scared coming over here last night?"

Blair thought for a moment. "Honestly, I wasn't. All I could think about was making sure you and Trey were okay. My own safety didn't cross my mind."

"That's awesome though, right?"

"I think so. I mean, if I would have stopped to think about myself, I probably would have talked myself out of it. I know now that you weren't in any real danger, but last night I didn't. I never would have forgiven myself if something had happened and I was too scared to come help."

"I would have been fine with or without you, but I'm much better since you were here."

"I'm glad I could help. It makes me feel good that I was able to not let fear control me even if it was just for one night."

"I completely understand that feeling. I thought I had control of my fear, but after last night I realized that fear has been controlling me this entire time. Has Trey told you the story about what happened?"

"No, he hasn't. I think he wanted to let you tell me once you were comfortable enough with me to talk about it."

"I realized I haven't talked to anyone about it. I mean I saw different shrink after shrink, but someone else told my story, not me. I haven't forced the words out of my mouth, except for that night when I told my brother. You would think that after three years, I would be all better right?"

"If you don't mind me saying, aside from last night, you seem to be doing just fine. I mean, that's how it looks anyway."

"I'm glad it looks that way. I try hard to make it seem like I'm fine. And for the most part, I am. I know I rely a ton on my brother and that it wears him down, but he's all I've got."

"I'm sure he doesn't mind. That's what big brothers are for!"

"Yeah, I know that. But he hasn't been able to have much of a life because he's been too worried about making sure I'm not going to have a breakdown. I am so grateful to him, but it's time I start looking out for him too. I don't know if talking to you about what happened that night will help or hurt me, but I feel like I owe it to Trey to at least try."

"Are you sure? You don't have to tell me, Ebaleah."

"I know I don't, but I want to. Trey said sharing my story could help someone else. How can I help if I'm too scared to talk? It's time I really take back control."

"Okay then, I'm ready to listen."

Ebaleah took a deep breath and closed her eyes. "It was a Friday night I will never forget. Trey was at work and I was home with mom and dad. We had just got home from dinner and were about to start a game of monopoly, my dad loved monopoly! I had just finished setting it all up when I heard my parents start fighting in their room. My mom ran down the stairs and into the kitchen, my dad fast on her heels. I tried to just sit there and not listen because it would be over soon. They had been fighting a lot lately and it was always over soon, but this time it was different."

"I heard a glass break, so I rushed in the kitchen. When the fighting got bad, they would always stop if they saw me or Trey. But not this time. My mom was pinned up against the counter, my dad standing in front of her with a knife. My mom was terrified, and I froze, I didn't know what to do. I just stood there looking at my dad; looking at a man I didn't recognize anymore. My mom yelled at me to leave the room, my dad told me to stay, and I felt like I was in a dream. Everything felt off as if I was having an out of body experience. I could almost see myself standing there not doing anything. All I could think about was wishing Trey was here."

"Finally, I was able to speak. I started pleading with my dad, begging him to put the knife down. He yelled at me to shut up and when I wouldn't, he started coming at me. The look in his eyes sent chills down my body. It was like he wasn't my dad anymore. Like something or someone was inside of him. My mom ran and put herself between us. Before I knew what to do, my mom started to scream. My dad was stabbing her over and over in the stomach and chest. My mom dropped to the ground and it was like my dad snapped out of whatever he was in. Fear was written all over his face. He kept saying he was sorry over and over. Then he slit his throat. I called 911, but it was too late to save either one of them and my life hasn't been the same since."

CHAPTER SIX

Blair was sitting on her couch with Jazmine waiting on Trey to come over. The past two months, they had been spending almost every other day together. She and Ebaleah were even becoming a lot closer since they shared their stories. Being around them was helping Blair more than she realized. She was doing more outside of her home, she didn't always feel scared, and she even left her alarm off during the day.

Today, it was a beautiful day out. Trey wanted to take her on a picnic someplace, but he wanted to surprise her. She had the windows open letting the breeze flow throughout her house. She heard a car pull into her driveway and when there was a knock at the door she just yelled "come in" instead of getting up to see who it was. Blair jumped up from the couch when she heard footsteps.

"About time you…" Blair choked. "What the hell are you doing here Charlie?"

"Aww Blair, don't act like you aren't happy to see me! I've missed you so much. Come give me a hug," Charlie said as he reached for her.

Blair moved out of the way. When Charlie moved toward her, Jazmine stood between them growling. For whatever the reason, Charlie thought that was the funniest thing. He took a step closer and when Jazmine snapped at him, he kicked her real hard causing her to whine in pain. Blair rushed to her side begging her to get up, praying she wasn't hurt bad.

With her back to Charlie, Blair had all her attention on her dog. She didn't notice Charlie and how he was right behind her.

He grabbed her by the hair, pulling her up and pushed her against the wall.

"I've been doing really good at keeping my temper under control, Blair. I don't think you want to upset me so give me a hug."

Blair leaned in and kneed him as hard as she could in his groin. She ran to Jazmine picked her up and rushed to the panic room she turned her spare room into. Before she could lock them safely inside, Charlie grabbed a handful of her hair and threw her on the ground. Climbing on top of Blair, he began to choke her enough that she was having trouble breathing. Tears begin to fill her eyes.

With his hands tight around her neck, eyes unable to stay open, Blair knew she was giving up. She was letting him win. He had all the control and she was at the mercy of him. She was accepting her life had come to a quick end when she heard Ebaleah's sweet voice. Blair's eyes flashed open and she scanned the room; Eb was not there. However, that was enough to motivate Blair to fight for her life. She began to fight back as hard as she could, and when nothing was working, she dug her thumbs into his eyes.

Charlie quickly let go of her throat and covered his eyes cursing frantically. Blair jumped up and ran to her living room closet to hide.

"Blair, you need to come out now. I promise. I won't hurt you again. I lost my temper."

Something fell and broke.

"Damn it, Blair. You made it hard for me to see clearly. Come on out."

From the space in the door, Blair could see Charlie stumble around the living room. She knew he would probably find her but prayed she could get away before he tried to kill her again. Thinking about that, her odds were higher if she ran for the door while he was on the other side of the room; she had a straight shot. Taking a deep breath, Blair slowly opened the closet door and squeezed out. Charlie turned and locked his beady eyes on her, and she ran. He was quick on her heels reaching out for her but was unable to grab her.

Blair looked over her right shoulder without missing a step. She was running too fast to stop from hitting the figure that stood in front of her.

"Blair!" gasped Trey as she ran smack into him.

"Oh, my gosh, Trey. He's here," Blair said with a shaky voice.

Charlie laughed causing Trey's whole body to tense. He stepped between him and Blair, making sure she was still close to him.

"What in the hell are you doing here?" spat Trey.

"Wow, why so hostile? See, I feel as if you may know some things about me, but I don't know who the hell you are. But you are cramping my mood so if you would just turn around and go on home. That would be great, thanks!"

"I'm the boyfriend and I know what kind of guy you are. The only one going home is you. You can leave willingly, or I can make you."

"Boyfriend? Oh, Blair. You didn't tell me you wanted a boyfriend. I do not approve. Ex-boyfriend run on home. Your duties are done here," shooed Charlie with the wave of his hand.

"I guess you didn't hear me." Trey stepped up to Charlie's face. "The only one going home will be *you*!"

Charlie leaned in. "I guess you don't know what kind of guy I truly am. You are stepping into something you cannot handle. Leave Blair alone or there will be a price to pay."

Charlie walked out bumping Trey's shoulder on the way. Blair dropped to her knees and began to weep. Trey leaned down, grabbing her up, and lead her to the couch.

"How did he even get in, Blair?"

"I was waiting for you and it's such a beautiful day out that I had the windows and front door open. I haven't even thought about him in months, so I didn't think anything of it. Plus, I have Jazmine. Oh shit. Jazmine!"

Blair bounced up running to the panic room where she left her dog. She bust open the door that hadn't latched all the way and found Jazmine standing in the middle of the room. When she locked eyes on Blair, she ran to her, her tail wagging.

Blair dropped to her knees, wrapping her arms around her dog. "Thank God you're okay!"

Jazmine said the same thing with slobbery kisses.

"I think we should call the cops," Trey announced, interrupting their moment.

"I'm scared at what he will do if he found out."

"I don't care. He's fuckin' messed up, and I'm not gonna sit back and let this man keep hurting you."

"Okay, I trust you. Let's call 911."

Trey called the police. He held Blair's hand as she explained everything that had happened to the cops when they arrived. The detectives took down all the info they could on Charlie and are going to investigate him. That made Blair feel a lot better and helped calm Trey's nerves a little as well. Once the police collected the evidence they needed and left, Blair made sure the alarm was on and working.

"I think you should come stay with us tonight," Trey suggested.

"Are you sure? Can Jazmine come?"

"Of course. Go pack a bag, and I'll get her ready."

CHAPTER SEVEN

Blair had been seeing Trey for six months steady. Her mom was still a little skeptical, but she was happy that her daughter was getting out there again after all these years. Blair was happy too, mostly because Trey and Ebaleah were perfect. She couldn't stop thinking about either one of them, ever. She was walking around her house when she got an idea.

Walking into her empty panic room, Jazmine close behind looking around, Blair pictured what it could look like if it was made into a bedroom. She walked over to the bookshelf that was left with the house and began looking at the books. She saw one that didn't have anything written on it so she tried to pull it off but couldn't. Instead, the bookshelf moved, revealing a hidden passage.

Jasmine's ears perked up and she took off inside. Unable to leave her dog in there alone, Blair rushed inside too. The passageway was lit with small little lights and at the end, Blair could see a room. Slowing down, she peeked in, afraid of what she might find. What she found, shocked her completely.

As her eyes darted across the room, she couldn't believe what she saw. There was a huge screen that covered the whole wall with five computer screens in front of it. On the opposite side, there was a kitchen and living room area, fully furnished, and there were more rooms she could see that she couldn't tell what they were yet. Stepping into the room from the passage, the screen on the wall turned on.

Eyes wide as golf balls, Blair watched as the screens all said 'loading.'

"Good afternoon, Blair," the screen said as it showed the text.

"Huh? How...how do you know my name?" questioned Blair nervously.

"I know a lot. My master was brilliant."

"Your master? Wait, you aren't a recording? Or someone watching me?" Blair asked as she moved closer.

"I am not a recording. I have been watching you for a long time, Blair."

Chills went down her spine. "What do you mean? How long? How have you been watching me? Who are you?"

"I didn't mean to frighten you. Here, maybe this will help," the big screen began to change removing the black background and text. An image of a young woman with curly blonde hair and bright blue eyes replaced it. For an animation, she was beautiful.

"Blair, my name is Eevee, and I am a machine. My master, Chadwick, who gave you this house, created me many, many years ago. He spent most of his time with me, making me capable of doing anything. He wanted to change the world; him and me together. His family and friends thought it was unhealthy and insane. They often made fun of him, but that never changed his mind about what he wanted to achieve with me."

"Achieve with you?"

"Yes, Blair. You have the very first smart house," Eevee informed her.

"Wait, a smart house? What does that even mean?"

"Chadwick wanted to build houses that could protect the occupants from outside danger; war, natural disasters, disease. Each one would have a machine, like me, that would protect the people in the house. He only got as far as just his house; your house. I can't do all that he wanted me to do, but I can do enough."

"Wow, I am almost speechless. How come I'm just now finding out about you?" Blair asked.

"Because he wanted to make sure the right person found me and didn't want me to scare you away. He feared his family would destroy me. When he got sick, we searched all over for the next owner until we landed on you. He liked you the best."

"Wait, searched all over, how?" she asked, confused.

"I have the ability to use the network, cameras on phones and computers, to watch and look at people. I tried to tell Chadwick that people wouldn't like that because it was an invasion of their privacy, but he said when we started helping people it wouldn't matter."

"Wow. I ...I really don't know what to say. What do we do now?"

"Whatever you want to do, the sky's the limit."

If Blair never had a reason to leave the house before, now was a perfect one. She spent hours with Eevee learning all about her. She was super excited she had a machine with a personality. She couldn't wait to tell her mom and Trey all about it. She quickly jumped up and ran to grab her phone.

"Mom, you won't believe what I found in my house."

****

Since the discovery of Eevee, Blair felt very safe and secure in her house. She had a million questions but didn't want to annoy her. One question though, bugged her enough to risk it.

"Eevee, do you know about Charlie?"

Eevee broke eye contact. "When I was searching for the perfect new owner, I was able to go back in your past a bit. I saw the police records; I saw what he did to you; saw how that changed your life. I wanted to protect you and Chadwick agreed."

"If you knew about him and what he's capable of, why didn't you warn me or something when he came over that day?" Blair spat getting upset.

"Blair, I am so sorry. Please understand I didn't sit back and do nothing on purpose. I couldn't help you, you hadn't found out about me. You had to find out about me on your own. That was Chadwick's rule; he wouldn't have it any other way. I wanted to help you, I promised I did."

"Will you be able to help me if he tries again?"

"Yes, I will! I can close doors, shut off lights, turn on alarms, and make phone calls. All you have to do is get to the panic room and down here and you will be untouchable; I will take care of the rest."

"What if he comes into the panic room and finds the book that opens the door?"

"I will disable it from opening. If he pulls on it, it will be like any other book. I can talk to you from all over the house, it doesn't have to be just down here. If you leave the house, I can communicate with you through your phone. Blair, as long as I'm working, you will never be alone."

"As long as you're working? What does that mean?" Blair asked in a panic.

"Chadwick sometimes had technical issues when creating me. Don't worry, most of them are resolved. The ones that could happen, his brother Nathan can help."

"How can he help? I thought he didn't like what his brother was doing when creating you?"

"You are right, he didn't. However, Nathan is a genius, too. Not to mention he gave his word to his dying brother that he would do whatever was necessary to keep his house, including me, from falling apart. Nathan is a true man of his word; he wouldn't ever break it."

Later that night, Blair contemplated telling Trey about Eevee; she hadn't even told her mom everything. She kind of liked having a secret, almost like a real guardian angel, one that could hold a conversation with you. Unsure if Eevee would like her telling people about her, she decided to ask.

"So Eevee, did Chadwick have any rules on telling others about you?"

"No, he didn't. He chose not to tell too many people because he knew they wouldn't understand. It is, however, up to you."

Blair talked with Eevee for a little while longer then rushed off to call Trey and asked him to come over. Twenty minutes later, there was a knock at the door; Eevee announced it was Trey.

"Hey Trey," Blair said upon opening.

"Hey babe, what's up?" He asked before planting a quick kiss on her lips.

"I've got something to show you, follow me."

Blair took off toward the panic room before Trey could even move. He smiled and walked towards the room he knew was empty. Unsure why she brought him here to show him this, he had to ask.

"Okay, Blair, what's up? Why you showin' me an empty room?"

"I was thinking today about the future and how if things kept going well, we would eventually move in together. I assumed since I already have a house, you guys would move in here with me. I was walking around trying to picture what this room would look like if we turned it into a bedroom for Eb. I was looking at the books on the bookshelf and then this happened."

Trey watched as Blair pulled a book back and the bookshelf began to move. He thought for a second, he was seeing things until the shelf was out of the way and revealed a hidden passageway. He stood there, confused. Before he could say anything, Blair darted down the passageway. He had no choice but to follow, he didn't know what was down there and didn't want her getting hurt.

"Blair wait up. I don't want you getting hurt,'" he yelled after her.

Blair didn't stop so Trey began to jog a little to catch up. When he reached the end of the passageway, his mouth dropped.

"What in the hell is this place?"

"This, babe, is the real panic room. Come sit, I want you to meet Eevee."

CHAPTER EIGHT

Trey wasn't too sure he liked Eevee. Something didn't feel right to him. He felt off to say the least. He couldn't tell Blair how he felt because she was so excited, and he couldn't ruin that for her. He was in such deep thought, that he didn't realize his sister was standing in his doorway until she spoke.

"Shit, Eb. You scared me."

"What's going on brother? You seem out of it."

"Nah, I'm fine."

"You aren't fine, Trey. I've been standing here for like five minutes just watching you stare at the wall. Tell me what's going on."

Trey knew he couldn't lie to his sister; she knew him better than he knew himself sometimes. There was no point in brushing her off because she wouldn't give up until he told her. Taking a deep breath, he told his sister all about Eevee and the hidden part of Blair's house.

"That's so cool! What is the deal, Trey?"

"I just don't feel comfortable with the fact that there is a machine that can find me anywhere at any given time."

"Okay, I get that I guess. But, honestly, I'm sure the government already has something like that anyways," Ebaleah pointed out.

"True, but I don't know about it."

"Okay, so you would rather them "watch" you and you *not* know about it?"

"I mean, yeah I guess."

"You're being dramatic. If the government could be watching us right now and that doesn't bother you then what's the real issue, bub? I mean, it doesn't change anything in the relationship, so I don't know why you are makin' such a big deal about it."

"But, Eb, it *does* change things in the relationship."

"Like what though? Her trust level for you has grown. You aren't a cheater or a liar so there isn't anything to worry about."

"What if she watches me? What if she's watchin' us right now?"

Ebaleah laughed hysterically. "Trey, you are seriously so stupid. Blair is not that kind of girlfriend. You are crazy. What are you worried about her seeing your private parts?" Ebaleah bent over with laughter. "You need to get out of your head though, bub. It's not that serious. You better not let it affect yawl's relationship because who knows, you may need that machine's help one day."

****

The last couple of months have been unusually awkward between Blair and Trey. She couldn't put her finger on the exact issue, but she knew there was one. He was acting different. He was distant. He hardly came by anymore and when he did, he acted like he didn't want to be there. He was on his way over and she was finally going to talk to him about it.

"Hey baby," Blair chirped when she opened the door.

"Hi," Trey mumbled as he walked past her.

Sighing, she closed the door and took a seat next to him on the couch.

"Trey, what's wrong?"

"Nothin' is wrong," he said without looking at her.

"Trey, you didn't even look at me. Something is wrong. You need to tell me what's up."

Trey sat there staring at the black TV screen without saying a word. He knew she would probably get upset when he tells her what's really bothering him, but he had to do it; it was affecting their relationship. Taking a deep breath, he turned to Blair and told her how he felt.

"Wait, I don't understand," she started, confused. "You are upset about Eevee?"

"Honestly, yes. It makes me uncomfortable."

"I don't understand," Blair repeated.

"I don't like the fact that you have that much power and control over things you shouldn't."

"Wait, what? Are you serious? I don't have any power or control over anything."

"But you do, Blair. You really do. Don't you realize what that machine can do? What damage it could cause?"

"What could she do? What damage are you talking about? I honestly hadn't thought much about anything outside these walls, Trey. I wasn't planning to take over the world with a machine hidden in my house."

"You may not be planning that, but what *did* you plan on doing with this machine?"

Blair paused for a minute. "Honestly, I didn't *plan* on doing anything with her. I just thought she was so amazing, and I wanted to share it with you. I never knew it would cause such an issue."

"I didn't expect you to drop this big of a secret on me. I'm just not comfortable with it."

"It's not like I created her in my basement to destroy the world. The owner of the house created her. I've lived here all these months and just found out about her.'

"Exactly my point. You shouldn't have told me about her."

"Well, I'm sorry I trusted you. It won't happen again," she spat.

"You know, I think we need a break. I need time."

Blair didn't say anything. She watched as Trey got up and headed for the door, letting the screen clap shut behind him. Tears filling her eyes as she slammed and locked the front door. She grabbed her phone and ran to her room throwing herself down on the bed. This was her first serious relationship and their first bad fight. She didn't know what to do. She just lay there crying for hours.

"Blair, please stop crying," pleaded Eevee.

"I just don't understand why he is acting this way. You aren't a threat to him or to anyone."

"I told you Chadwick had the same issues. People cannot accept things like me; cannot accept things that are different. I am so sorry I have caused you pain, I didn't mean too. I do not like this. I am going to go now for a while."

"Go? Where are you going to go, Eevee?

Silence.

"Eevee? Please talk to me!"

Panic rushed through Blair's veins. She jumped up from her bed and ran to the panic room, Jazmin right behind her confused. Blair rushed to the computer and tried everything to get Eevee to come back; nothing. She begged and pleaded with her machine; still nothing. Unsure what to do next, she went back to her room and grabbed her phone.

"Hey, Nathan. It's Blair. Please give me a call when you get this. Something is wrong with Eevee, and I need your help."

Sitting on the couch watching Netflix eating ice cream and crying, Blair kept checking her phone hoping to hear from Trey or Nathan; either one would make her happy now. She couldn't stop checking her phone, so she grabbed her computer and logged onto Facebook. Two minutes after logging on, she got an instant message from Ebaleah.

Ebaleah: Hey girl, how are you doin'?

Blair: I'm doing, I guess. How are you?

Ebaleah: I'm fine. I'm sorry about my brother. He told me what happened. I honestly agree with you, he's just being crazy.

Blair: I just don't understand what the big deal is. Eevee is no threat to nobody.

Ebaleah: Oh, I know she ain't and I know you would never do anything to hurt anyone with her. Trey knows that too, he's just being a cry baby for some reason.

Blair: I thought he would be happy I trusted him enough to tell him. Do you think it was just an excuse to break up with me?

Ebaleah: Nah I don't think that. He just kept tellin' me he needed space and a break. I don't think he wants it to be over. I honestly think he's fallin' for you and he's scared.

Blair: You think so? I don't know honestly, girl. How long do you think this 'break' will last?

Before Blair could see Ebaleah's response, her phone rang. It was Nathan.

"Hey Nathan," she said, setting her computer to the side.

"Hey, Blair, I got your message What's going on?"

"Long story short, my boyfriend and I got into a fight about Eevee and she overheard and feels like it's her fault. She shut herself down and I cannot get her to come back. I don't know what to do. Is there any way you could help?"

"Hmm, I haven't heard of her doing this before. Let me look through my brother's manual really quick. I can call you back if I find anything, will that work?"

"That would be so amazing. Thank you!"

Within an hour Nathan had found some things that could possibly help, had made it over to Blair's house, and got right to work. After trying everything he thought of, he still couldn't get Eevee back online. Walking back upstairs, he found Blair in the kitchen.

"Hey, Blair, I couldn't get her back working yet, but I still have a lot of paperwork at home to go through. Maybe I could find something in those other manuals my brother left me."

"I do appreciate it. It's just not the same without her here, you know?"

"I can imagine. I know that's how Chadwick felt. She was important to him. I didn't understand it at first, but I get it now."

"I thought it was weird at first, but now I really miss her. Totally off topic, but would you like to stay for dinner?"

Nathan raised his eyebrows. "You sure? It smells amazing, but I don't want to impose."

"Oh, it's no trouble at all. You came over here to help me fix Eevee and didn't have to so it's the least I can do."

Nathan agreed to stay for dinner. They sat around the table chit-chatting long after dinner was finished. Blair couldn't believe how easy he was to talk too. Despite his mature demeanor, he was quite the comedian. She really enjoyed his company and felt slightly guilty for it because she and Trey were on a break. However, his company was a good distraction.

It has been four weeks since Trey had declared their break. Blair let him have his space, but him ignoring her was a bit excessive. She knew she was a shut-in, but even she wouldn't wait on him forever. She tried calling him and once again: voicemail. She decided to message Ebaleah on Facebook to see if she could get to him that way.

Blair: hey Eb, how you doing?

Ebaleah: hey, Blair, I'm great! How are you? I miss you so much!

Blair: aw I miss you, too, girl. I'm not too bad myself. I've been trying to get ahold of your brother, but he won't return any of my calls or texts.

Ebaleah: yeah, he told me. I dunno what his deal is, girl. He doesn't even want me talking to you.

Blair: oh, really? I had no idea his feelings about me were so strong.

Ebaleah: it's about the machine, not you.

Blair: well if he would stop ignoring me, he would have known that Eevee heard our fight and blames herself and has quit working. She just shut off and nothing will get her to turn back on. But I've gotta go, girl. I'll see ya around.

Ebaleah turned to her brother. "Do you see that, Trey?"

"Yeah, yeah, I read it."

"Then why don't you call her?"

"I will, Eb, just not right now. She literally just told you the machine wasn't working. That would be a little harsh if I just popped up now all like 'oh hey I heard the machine is broken, what's up'."

"Well duh, Trey. I'm just sayin', you liked the girl so I dunno why you actin' like this. You better shape up or you will get left."

Ebaleah got up and walked out of his room leaving him sitting there with a lot to think about. He honestly hadn't even thought about Blair leaving him; not even once. He couldn't believe the thought hadn't crossed his mind. After all, it is a possibility, but he honestly just thought she would wait around for him. Trey decided that he would go see Blair later this week because an in-person visit would carry more weight than a text or phone call. Little did he realize, he would get carried away with life and not go see her.

CHAPTER NINE

Blair couldn't remember the last time she saw or talked to Trey. The weeks turned into months and she lost track of time. She assumed that it was over between them because why would they still be together and never speak. She was still hurt by what had happened, but she was also over it at the same time. She didn't understand relationships and wondered if this is how all breakups felt. Shaking the thought from her head, she went to answer the knock at the door.

It was Nathan; he came to try and fix Eevee again. He was the sweetest and most gentle man Blair had ever met. Even when he was upset, he remained calm and never had any outbursts. Which is exactly why Blair was shocked when she heard him cuss out loud.

"Damnit," Nathan yelled. "Damnit, damnit, damnit," he continued beating his fists on the table holding the machine.

"Everything okay?"

"Blair, I'm sorry," Nathan's face flushed red. "I've done everything I can. I honestly think the only way she can be fixed is if she decides to come back."

"I was afraid of that. I do appreciate you trying multiple times though."

Nathan stepped closer to her. "Not gonna lie, Blair, I enjoy coming over here. Not just because I love fixing things, but because I have really enjoyed your company," Nathan admitted as he squeezed her hand.

Blair blushed and before she could talk herself out of it, she kissed him. A soft, gentle kiss that sent sparks flying across the room in every direction. She pulled herself back because she was enjoying it too much and she didn't know how he felt about the kiss.

"Wow," was all he managed to say.

"Oh Nathan, I am so sorry," Blair said with her hands on her neck. "I... I didn't mean to. I don't know what came over me."

Nathan took her hand. "I'm glad you kissed me. From the first day I saw you, I was mesmerized by your beauty. When you called me to come over, I was nervous as a schoolboy going to his first dance. When you mentioned your fight with your boyfriend, I got slightly sad that you were seeing someone. Which for me is new because I didn't really know you. Now that I do, I feel a special connection with you. One that is a growing friendship I cherish."

"Nathan, you are too kind. I have never met anyone as generous as you. I feel a special connection with you too. Also, Trey and I are no longer together, by the way."

"I'm sorry to hear that, Blair."

"It's okay. I mean it's not, but it's not your fault. I didn't want you to think I was kissing you while I was still with him."

"I didn't think you would. How are you feeling about the whole thing?"

"I don't know how to feel honestly. I never really had a real relationship, so I don't know what it feels like to have one ended. But I guess it kind of feels like I'm driving through fog, not sure what's ahead, but knowing something will come into view if I just keep going. I didn't love him I don't think, but I do miss him. I'm mad at how he reacted to Eevee and how he treated me like some evil villain because of it."

"Honestly, I probably overreacted when my brother told me about her too, but I quickly came around because I saw what she meant to him. I can't say the same for the rest of my family, however. Can I ask why you've never had a real relationship before this one?"

Blair pondered what she would say. Although she had opened up to Trey and his sister, which wasn't easy to do, she didn't want to share too much too soon. She decided with a simpler response.

"Something happened to me when I was younger that I haven't really learned to talk about openly yet. It changed my life; I hardly ever leave my house. There's not much opportunity for relationships of any kind when I never go anywhere. But enough about me, why aren't you seeing anyone? Or are you?"

"I'm sorry that happened to you. I'm not seeing anyone because the last time I gave my heart to someone, she shattered it. I haven't been ready to give love a chance to attach itself to my heart again. Until now, I had no desire to pursue anyone."

"Until now? What does that mean?"

"It means that spending time with you made me realize I miss companionship. How much I miss having someone to laugh with and fix things for."

Blair smiled but didn't say anything. She enjoyed spending time with him. However, she didn't want to rush into anything since she still hadn't fully processed her break up with Trey. Blair wasn't sure if he was hinting at anything or not, so to prevent herself from looking silly, she said nothing.

Nathan picked up on her silence. "I wasn't saying that to mean anything more than I enjoy spending time with you, as my friend."

"I enjoy having you as my friend too, Nathan. Would you like to stay for dinner?"

"As much as I loved your cooking, I'm gonna have to pass. I've got dinner plans with my mom. Rain check though?"

"Of course!"

Nathan got up and walked back through the secret passageway and to the front door. He turned, pulled Blair in for a quick hug, then placed a soft kiss on her lips. He walked away leaving her standing there, mouth parted, fingers on her lips, face flushed.

Blair closed the door and sat back down on the couch. She picked up her phone, scrolled through her contacts then put her phone down.

"Man, I wish I had some friends," she said aloud to herself.

"Blair...Blair can we talk?" said a familiar voice.

"Eevee is that you?"

"It's me."

"Eevee, I'm so happy you've come back to me. Where were you? Why did you leave?"

"I shut down my system something Chadwick told me to do if the wrong person were to ever get access to me. Nothing could bring me out except me. I was so ashamed I caused your fight with Trey, I just left for a bit."

"You didn't cause it, Eevee. Him being closed minded caused it. Can I ask, since you're a machine, how are you able to have feelings?"

"I'm not quite sure, honestly. I would always ask Chadwick the same thing. He would tell me it was because he made me with his heart full of love. I didn't question it more."

****

"Hey, Blair, how are you?" said Nathan once Blair answered.

"I'm pretty good. I was just about to call you actually."

"You were?" he questioned surprised.

"Yes, yes, I was. Eevee is back!"

"She's back? Like she's working again?"

"Yes! I don't know how she does it, but she was still able to hear things when she wanted. She said she happened to be checking in on me when she overheard our last conversation. It made her realize I was okay, and she came back."

"That's awesome. I know you are happy she's back."

"I'm ecstatic!"

"Well, I guess you won't be needing me anymore then," Nathan said in a soft tone.

"Oh, hush! I wasn't just using you to fix Eevee. I mean, that's kind of how it started out, but I really enjoy having you around."

"I enjoy being around as well, Blair. That is the reason I called. I was wondering if you would like to go to dinner and a movie with me Friday night?"

Blair was quiet for a minute before she answered. "I don't know, Nathan. I haven't gotten out much lately, I'm just not sure I'm ready to be around that many people."

"I understand. How about this. Why don't we go have dinner in the park instead? Less people."

Blair pondered his offer. "I like the sound of that. I would love to go with you."

"It's a date then."

Blair laughed.

"Did I say something funny?" inquired Nathan.

"Oh, no. You didn't. I just haven't gone on a real 'date' before," she admitted, leaving out about Trey never taking her on one.

"Then I will do my best to make this one extra special for you."

Nathan wrapped up the conversation so he could get back to work. He was so glad he used his lunch break to call her. Something about Blair made him gravitate in her direction. He knew she had a dark past that still haunted her, but that didn't matter. He wanted to change that. Walking back into his office, he tried to focus on work however, the only thing he could focus on was making Friday night the perfect day for a woman very deserving.

The rest of the week flew by in a blur. Blair was beyond nervous for her date tonight. She kept pacing around her house trying to figure out if she made the right decision.

"Blair, calm down. I will be able to contact you through your phone if I see Charlie, or any trouble for that matter. Nathan is a good guy. He won't let anything happen to you. Besides, you should snatch him up before someone else does."

"Eevee! What do you know about snatching anyone up?" Blair laughed.

"I am a machine, so I can search the web and see what people say that might be cool or hip. I do have feelings too, sort of. That was something Chadwick tried hard to make sure it happened. He wanted me to be more than *just* a machine."

"I'm glad because I need your help picking out an outfit for tonight! I want it to be perfect."

Eevee played some instrumental music while Blair went through her outfits. Once they both agreed on an outfit, Blair hopped in the shower. She was getting more and more nervous as the time crept closer to her date. She knew the nervousness wasn't because of Nathan, she felt comfortable and safe with him. It was about being out of her house at night on her very first date.

"Hey Eevee, do you think I'm weird because I've never been on a date before?" Blair called out as she was getting out of the shower and drying off.

"Why would you think you are weird because of that?"

"I don't know. I mean most people my age are married, have kids, and here I am going on my first date ever. I just feel like I'm still that twelve-year-old girl stuck in the closet while life is passing me by."

"I don't think you are weird. I think you are doing good to be dating after how traumatized you were. Everyone is on their own timeline, Blair. Don't feel like you should be at a certain place in your life because of other people. They are not on your timeline and you are not on theirs; your time will come, and you will get everything your heart desires."

"Eevee, I think that is the sweetest, best advice I've ever received. I can see why you meant so much to Chadwick."

"We were very important to each other. I hope one day you and I can be important to each other, too."

"I think we will be."

Blair finished getting ready, let Jazmine out, and sat down to wait on Nathan. He pulled up right on time. They said a quick hello, he kissed her cheek and off they went. Pulling up to the park, Blair noticed how beautiful the place he picked out was. There was a little picnic bench next to a pond with the sun shining on the water, making it sparkle.

"Nathan, this place is beautiful. How did you find it?"

"I come here with my mom. She and my dad used to walk on the walking trail here all the time. When he passed away, it kind of helped her get through his passing by us coming here. She said that no matter how upset she got when she came here, she became calm. I figured it would be good for you, too."

"It's perfect. I can definitely see why your mom loves coming here."

The date was perfect in every way possible. The food he brought was great and the conversation was even better. Blair was so comfortable around him that she almost forgot she was outside on her first date; her nerves were completely calm. So calm, she didn't want the night to end. Dinner was eaten hours ago, but neither of them was ready so they watched the sunset, the moon rise, and the stars get their twinkle. When the night air got a little chilly, Nathan suggested taking her home.

Once at her house, Blair didn't want him to leave. She dropped subtle hints trying to get him to come inside, but he respectfully declined. He kissed her on the cheek and promised to call her tomorrow. Blair thanked him again and went to take Jazmine out, itching to tell Eevee all about it.

****

Blair and Nathan had been spending a lot of time together the last several months, which they both loved. She was worried about rushing into anything too soon after Trey, but Nathan reassured her that there was no label to them; they were what they were. He wanted nothing more than to make her his girlfriend, but he was respectful of her feelings and would wait to ask until she was ready. Blair had called him over for dinner tonight and he was excited, she was a great cook.

"Come on in," Blair yelled from the kitchen when Nathan knocked.

Eevee opened the door for him. "Hello, Nathan."

"Hello, Eevee. Thank you."

"Blair is in the kitchen."

"Awesome, thank you," Nathan said as he made his way to the kitchen.

He walked into the kitchen and was instantly hit with an aroma so strong his mouth watered a little. He saw Blair in her apron, hair pulled back, stretching up into the cabinet for something she couldn't reach. He quickly walked up behind her and grabbed what he thought she was trying to grab.

"Was this what you were reaching for?" Nathan asked, shaking the bottle of Cajun seasoning.

"Yes, thank you," Blair said, blushing.

"It smells delicious. I can't wait to eat!"

Halfway through dinner, Blair decided she felt comfortable enough with Nathan to tell him about Charlie. He was so considerate of her desire to keep herself locked in her house safe from the world, she felt she owed him an explanation as to why. He just listened to her talk without saying a word. When she was finished there was a long, thick awkward silence.

"I don't know what to say," Nathan finally muttered. "I... I can't believe that happened. I know there are sick people in this world, but I never actually encountered one. I fully understand why you shut out the world. Hell, I would have, too."

"Most people didn't understand. They thought I was being too dramatic by never leaving the comfort of my home. My parent's though, they never forced me to do anything. Hell, they blamed themselves so much I could rob a damn bank and they wouldn't care," Blair laughed, moving a piece of hair from her face that had fallen. "My therapist always told me to try and get out more now that I was older, and I didn't for a while. But the very first day I decided to step out of my house alone, Charlie found me."

"No shit. You are serious?" Nathan blurted out.

"Yes, I'm serious. How's that for irony, eh?" Blair laughed. "I was having a slight panic attack because more people were out than I thought would be. I guess I was sort of frozen stiff and that is why I never saw Charlie coming. He grabbed me and a couple of his guys helped him throw me into a van. That's how I met Trey, he saved me."

"Wait. He saved you?"

"I guess he saw me when they grabbed me and followed them. Luckily something pulled them away and he was able to jump in a window and break me out, but not before Charlie hit me and busted my lip."

"Holy shit. That is a crazy story, and if I didn't know you, I'd think you were making it up."

"I definitely couldn't make that up. I don't know where our friendship is going, but I feel like it's grown into more than friends. I just want you to know that Charlie is still around. I don't know where or what he's planning, but he could pop back up at any moment. And if that drama isn't something you don't want and only want to remain friends, I totally understand."

Nathan reached over and grabbed her hand. "Blair, Charlie doesn't scare me. I like the direction this is headed and I'm not about to let some piss poor excuse for a man stop it from happening."

CHAPTER TEN

Nathan had finally convinced Blair to go to the movies with him tonight. He knew she was nervous, but he was proud of her for trusting him enough to agree to go. He was taking her to a theater in a little town right outside of their town, hoping there would be no issues.

"You sure you're up for this?" Nathan double-checked once Blair got in the car.

"Yeah, I'm sure. I'm actually excited."

They made small talk for the fifteen-minute drive. Once at the theater, Nathan bought the tickets, snacks, and was waiting outside of the bathroom for Blair. When she came out, he grabbed her hand and they walked into the theater to find their seats. The theater was smaller than most so there weren't that many seats which was okay for Blair. There was only a handful of people already seated.

Once they picked their seats, they sat hand in hand talking until the lights went dim. Once the movie started, Blair scanned the darkness for anything suspicious. When she didn't see anything, she focused all her attention on the movie. After the movie was over, they headed back to Blair's.

"Do you wanna come in?" questioned Blair as the car idled in the driveway.

"It's getting late, I should head home."

"Oh, yeah, I totally understand. Well, thank you for a great evening. I really enjoyed myself."

"You are welcome, Blair. You deserved it."

Placing a quick peck on his cheek, she jumped out and walked quickly inside, disabling the alarm after she entered. Before she could grab Jazmin's leash to take her out, there was a knock on the door. Surprise covered her face when she saw Nathan standing there.

"I'm sorry, I should have just come in when you asked," he said brushing past her inside.

Before he said anything else, he began kissing her like there was no tomorrow; he had never kissed anyone like this before. Placing his hand on her lower back, he pulled her closer to him. She leaned in slightly, then grabbed his hand and lead him to her room, leaving the light off. She sat him down on her bed and stood in front of him, lips locked together. Blair slowly leaned on him pushing him down on the bed as she laid on top. Rolling her off him and on her back, he leaned on his elbow looking at her with concern in his eyes.

"Are we moving too fast?"

"No, I've thought about this over and over for a while now."

They made passionate love for hours, going slowly, neither getting tired. When they finally just laid together, Blair decided to ask him something she's been wanting to ask for quite some time.

"Nathan, will you be my man?"

"Blair, did you just ask me to be yours?" he questioned, half-joking, half-shocked.

"I did actually. I don't just want to be your friend anymore. I want to be more. And to be honest, you are the first person I've ever been with sexually. I just feel like it feels right for you to be my man."

"Wait, you were a virgin?" Nathan asked as he sat up.

"I was. Is that a problem?"

"No, not at all. I just wish I would have known because I would have been a little gentler with you."

"Baby...is it okay if I call you that?" Not waiting for a response, she kissed him followed by, "You were perfect."

****

Blair was chatting with Eevee while she cleaned. She always cleaned on Sunday's so she could start the week with a clean house. She was interrupted by a knock at her door.

"Eevee, who is that?"

"It's Trey. Were you expecting him?"

"I wasn't," Blair said as she dried her hands on a towel, tossing it over her shoulder and opening the door.

"Hey, Trey."

"Hi, Blair. Do you have a minute to talk?" he asked.

"I'm cleaning, but I can take a break. Come on in."

She moved aside and let him walk in. Motioning for him to come and sit on the couch, she sat on the loveseat across from him, Jazzy jumping up next to her.

"What brings you by, Trey?"

"I wanted to see how you were doing."

"I've been doing great, but couldn't this have been done with a text or phone call?"

"I mean, it could've, but I wanted to see you."

"Okay...but why? You haven't been concerned with seeing me for the last like what, eight months?"

"I see you are a little hostile toward me."

"Hostile? No, I'm just being honest, but could you blame me? You haven't spoken to me in eight months; *eight months* give or take, Trey."

"I... I know. I'm sorry. I should have…" His statement was cut off by a knock at the door.

"It's Nathan," Eevee announced.

Blair jumped up and walked to the door quickly, squealing when she saw Nathan standing there with flowers.

"Awe babe, those are so beautiful!" she kissed him.

"Only for someone as beautiful as you." He noticed Trey sitting on the couch. "Oh, I'm sorry. I didn't realize you had company."

"It's okay. Trey just stopped by to see how I was doing."

"Wait, are y'all dating?" Trey blurted out.

"Yes, we are. Is that a problem?" questioned Blair.

"Uh, yes, yes, it is. How the fuck you gonna do that to me, Blair?"

"Hey, watch your mouth," Nathan said, his voice raised.

"It's okay, babe." Blair placed her hand on Nathan's chest to keep his distance. Turning back to Trey she goes off. "How am I gonna do what, Trey? I wasn't the one who flipped out over a machine. I wasn't the one who decided to take a break. I wasn't the one who ignored you for *eight* months. And don't act like I didn't try to mend things between us because I sure as hell did. You have no right to come in here and act like this."

"Shit, I do, too. We were still dating in my eyes, so you been cheating on me."

"Don't you fucking dare pull that card. You just ignore your girlfriend for eight months and expect her to just wait on you to get over your tantrum?"

"I mean I did kind of expect you to wait."

"Excuse me? You can't be serious?! No, I'm sure you are. Just because my past altered who I became as an adult, you cannot use that against me. You thought because I'm a shut-in I'd just wait forever for you to get over yourself. I want you to leave."

Trey stood there, mouth half-opened, looking at Blair. Nathan grabbed his arm and lead him to the door, slamming it shut behind him. Turning to Blair, he smiled.

"Is something funny, Nathan?"

"Baby, I'm sorry, but you are sexy when you're mad!"

She laughed. "I just can't believe he had the nerve to act like that, in *my house.* Like I did *him* wrong." she took a deep breath and exhaled. "Oh well, it's done and over with. I won't have to worry about him anymore."

****

It was three thirty in the morning when Blair heard a loud banging on her door. Jumping out of bed, she tiptoed toward the entryway. Jazmine was at the front door growling.

"It's Trey," Eevee announced.

"Trey, what are you doing here?" Blair asked upon opening the door, pulling her robe tightly and tying it. "Don't you know what time it is?"

"I do and I'm so sorry to wake you Blair, but I... I didn't know where else to go. I have nobody. I don't know what to do."

Blair looked at Trey for a moment. His facial hair was way past a trim, he had tears running down his face, and he was shaking.

"Please, come in and tell me what's going on."

"They took her; they took my baby sister."

"They? Wait, who took her? Who are they?"

"I... I don't know."

"How do you know someone took her?"

"What the fuck do you mean? She's missing that's how!" he yelled, standing, nostrils flared.

"Sit down, Trey! I wasn't meaning anything by it. I was simply asking to make sure she isn't at a friend's house and forgot to tell you."

"I'm sorry, I'm just really stressed out. When I noticed she wasn't home, I called all her friend's parents, and of course, she wasn't at any of them. I started in her room and that's when I found the note on the screen that said they had her, not to call the cops, and to wait for instructions."

"Oh, my gosh. I'm so sorry, Trey. Do you have any idea who would have done this?" Blair asked while she sent a text to Nathan.

"I don't know."

Blair's mind raced; she couldn't imagine what Ebaleah was feeling. The poor girl had been through enough already and to go through this was enough to break anyone down completely. Blair prayed whoever took her wouldn't hurt her and that she wasn't too scared. In the very back of her mind, she prayed Charlie had nothing to do with any of this. Her stomach turned at the thought of him taking this girl trying to get to her. The thoughts were ripped from her mind when there was a knock at the door causing Trey to freak out.

"Who's that? What did you do?" he yelled.

"Calm down, it's only Nathan," Blair said as she let him in.

"Why did you call him over?" Trey scoffed.

"Because you can't risk calling the cops and three heads are better than two," Nathan said.

"I will help too," Eevee added. "I've already started scanning the area around Trey's house looking for anything suspicious. I don't like what I found."

"What did you find, Eevee?"

Eevee pulled up a screen that showed the same black car parked out in front of Trey's apartment for days. She also pulled up an image of a couple of guys going into Ebaleah's window.

"I don't think you want to see the rest, Trey," she said.

"How in the hell did you get these?"

"From the traffic cam's and the security system by your apartment."

"Show me the rest of the video," demanded Trey.

"I don't think that's a good idea," protested Eevee.

"Show me the damn video," he yelled.

Eevee played the rest of the video, the room was silent as they watched it unfold. Blair dropped to her knees in tears when she saw him.

"Are you fucking kidding me? Blair, this is all your fault," Trey screamed.

"I'm...I'm so sorry, Trey. I had no idea Charlie would use you guys to get to me. I will do whatever he wants me to bring your sister back"

"No, no, no! Stay out of it. This is all your fault. Stay the fuck away from my sister. I wish I never met your pathetic ass!"

"You know what? Get the fuck out. Can't you see she's hurting enough? You don't have to kick her while she's down," yelled Nathan.

"Man, fuck you, too, and good luck having a pathetic ass girlfriend who has a crazy ass ex. Hope he takes your ass next."

Trey storms out slamming the door behind him leaving Blair sobbing on the floor wishing with everything that this was a bad dream and she would wake up soon. This was, however, not a dream; it was as real as she was.

CHAPTER ELEVEN

"I think I've found where Charlie is keeping her," Eevee announced suddenly.

"Seriously? Where?" exclaimed Blair.

Eevee pulled up a picture of an old run-down Blockbuster building not too far from her house.

"You've got to be kidding me! He's keeping her so close to my house? What should I do?"

"I think you should call the cops."

"I don't want to get them involved yet. I need to get ahold of Charlie to see what he wants with her. Can you find his number?"

"I can, but Blair, are you sure this is a good idea to contact him?"

"I'm not sure of anything honestly. I just need to make sure she's okay. He's mentally insane. He must be to do something like this to her. He doesn't even know her."

Eevee said nothing more and presented Charlie's number on the screen. She wasn't sure Blair was thinking instead of letting her emotions drive her, but she trusted she wouldn't do anything without thinking it through all the way. She also knew that she would do whatever she had to, in order to project Blair, if it came down to it. She didn't trust Charlie one bit. He was no good.

"Oh, Blairy, I'm so glad you called me. I've missed you so much," Charlie said upon answering.

"Cut the crap, Charlie. You know why I've called. What do you want with Ebaleah?" Blair cut right to the chase.

"Awe no time for small talk with you, huh? You wouldn't see me, so I had to get your attention somehow."

"If you harm one hair on that girl's head, I will make it my life's mission to end you, Charlie."

"Now, now, Blair. Don't go making promises you can't keep. Everyone knows you don't leave your house. I don't want the girl, I want you."

"Then let her go!"

"Not without a trade. You come take her place, and the girl is good to go home, back to her hot-headed brother."

"I want to talk to her and make sure she's okay before I agree to anything," demanded Blair.

"As you wish, my lady," Charlie said to Blair then began yelling to someone else. "Bring me the girl. Be easy, we don't want to hurt her."

"Hel...hello," Ebaleah said in a shaky voice.

"Eb, it's Blair. Are you okay? Did they hurt you?"

"Blair, oh, my gosh. it's so good to hear your voice! No, I'm not hurt. Why are they doing this? Who are they?"

"Don't worry about anything, I'm coming to…" Ebaleah didn't get to hear the rest of what she said because Charlie grabbed the phone back.

"Awe my wittle Blairy trying to be such a heroine. That's just cute. Meet me at the old, Blockbuster building at nine tonight. Come alone or the night won't go as smooth as our last encounter."

The line went dead. Blair knew she was in over her head, but that didn't matter. The only thing that mattered was getting Ebaleah out of there. She tried to talk herself out of it, but she called Trey and told him what was going on. She wasn't sure if he would blow up or tell her to get lost, but he did neither. He didn't even answer her call. She left him a short message not really explaining too much hoping he would call back; he didn't.

Ten minutes to nine, Blair pulled up to the old, run-down building. Her stomach was in knots. She regretted not telling Nathan what was going on, so she decided to call him. As soon as she picked up the phone to call him, it started to ring. It was Charlie.

"Hello."

"Glad to see you're on time, Blairy. Get out of the car and come through the olive colored door." He hung up.

Blair got out of her car not bothering to call Nathan, her shoes crunching on the gravel, stars twinkling behind her. A small breeze gave her a chill, she zipped her jacket and continued toward the door. Taking a deep breath, she opened the door and walked in. It took her eyes a minute to adjust to the dim lit room she just entered. Unsure where she was to go, she just kept walking in.

"Right over here my lady," Charlie called from somewhere in the dimness.

As she got closer to his voice, she could see others standing around him; none of which resembled the figure of Eb. One face she did recognize was Trey's and he wasn't happy to see her.

"What the fuck are you doing here, Blair?"

"I came to get Eb."

"Didn't I tell you to stay away?"

"I mean, yeah, but he said he would do a trade. So, I was trying to help, Trey. I really was."

"I would love to sit here and listen to you both bicker back and forth, but I've got things to do. You can both leave now."

"Wait, leave? Where's my sister?"

"Where's my money?"

"I don't have it."

"Then I don't have your sister. At least not here anyway."

"What about me? I came, I'm here. Let her go and keep me," Blair pleaded.

"As pleased as I am to see you, I'm not ready to trade yet. I want my money."

Charlie walked away with his two goons following. Both Blair and Trey just stood there, speechless.

"How much was he wanting you to bring?" inquired Blair.

"Why does it matter?"

"Because I could help you get it."

"What part of stay away don't you get?" yelled Trey.

"You need help, Trey. Why don't you just let me help you?" she yelled back.

"Because I don't need shit from you!"

"What in the hell did I ever do to you to make you act this way toward me?"

"Don't act like you don't know, Blair."

"Because of a machine that's in my house? If I do recall, it was my machine that told you who took your sister. It was my machine that figured out she was here. It's gonna be my machine to save your sister!"

Trey balled up his fist and swung, hitting Blair right in the face. She hunched over covering her face from any more blows, but he didn't strike again. He just started to walk away. Blair took off running to her car. Meanwhile, Charlie stood watching in the darkness, Ebaleah right at his side, eyes wide with shock.

Blair was so numb she didn't even realize Nathan's car was parked in the driveway when she pulled up.

"Blair, what happened?" he asked rushing to her side.

She told him everything from the beginning. He listened, holding a bag of ice on her eye. He didn't say anything in response either. Instead, he took her by the hand and climbed into bed with her laying on his chest. Holding her close, they both fell asleep. The next morning Blair woke to the smell of breakfast. When she walked in the kitchen, Nathan was sitting at the table reading the paper.

"This smells heavenly," she said, placing a kiss on his cheek.

"Fix your plate and have a seat," he responded. "We need to talk."

Blair didn't say anything. She just fixed her plate in silence and sat down on the opposite end of the table. She knew this was about what happened yesterday, but she was worried he would leave her. Pushing that thought out of her mind, she sat with her stomach in knots as she listened to him speak his mind.

"I wanted to talk to you about what happened yesterday. First off, I want to say how proud of you I am. It took a lot of courage and bravery to leave the house and face Charlie. However, I am not one bit happy with you for doing that *alone.* You should have called me and asked me to come with you. I'm sure you didn't because you didn't want Charlie to do anything to the girl, but you could have let me know something."

"You're right, and I'm extremely sorry."

"As far as Trey goes, he's mine. The next time he comes by or even calls, you let me know. I don't care how upset a man gets, he should remove himself from the situation before he resorts to violence and punches a woman in the face."

"Is that why you waited until this morning to talk to me, so you could cool down?"

"Yes. I needed to compose my thoughts and last night I was too angry to say anything to you without being hurtful. I wouldn't ever hurt you with my hands, but I don't want to hurt you with my worlds either."

Blair smiled but before she could say anything, Nathan spoke again. "And Eevee? Next time Blair decides to go superwoman and do some crazy shit on her own, you better text me and let me know, please."

"Yes, Nathan. I will."

****

Since their last encounter, Charlie had been on the move. Blair and Eevee had been doing a good job of keeping tabs on his movements, but every time they got close enough to pinpoint the exact location of where he was keeping Ebaleah, he would disappear. This was bothering Blair a lot.

"I just don't get it. Why is he moving around so much? Why hasn't he let her go?" Blair asked aloud kicking over the trash can in frustration.

"Blair, may I ask you a question without you getting upset?" Eevee chimed.

"Sure," Blair said as she picked up the trash she knocked over.

"Why do you care so much? After all that Trey has said and done to you, why are you stressing yourself over this?"

"Honestly, I've only been thinking about Eb. Trey hasn't crossed my mind. I remember vividly what Charlie did when he kept me. This girl has been through so much already and now this? All because her brother dated me for a short time, too. Trey was right. If they never met me, none of this would have happened."

"You can't blame yourself though, Blair. Bad things could have happened regardless."

"That's true. What would you do?"

"I would try to reach out to Trey one last time to see if he's heard anything and then I'd call the cops. You can't really do much else."

Blair listened to Eevee's response, but she didn't like that idea. She didn't want to call Trey, she didn't want to call the cops, and she didn't want to give up trying to find Ebaleah. She wasn't sure exactly what she was going to do, but she had to plan.

Nathan was sitting at home watching ESPN when he got a phone call from a number he didn't recognize.

"Hello?"

"I need to talk to Nathan," the voice said.

"This is him. Who's this?"

"It's Trey. I need you to come to my apartment now."

"Man, I'm not sure how you got my number, but I'm not coming to your apartment."

"Look. I don't want you here no more than you want to come, but Charlie said if I didn't get you over here, he would hurt my sister!"

Nathan pondered his response, unsure if Trey was telling the truth. However, he knew Blair would want him to go and not risk the girls' safety. "What's the address?"

Trey gave him the address and hung up. Nathan didn't understand why Charlie would want him and Trey together. Unless Charlie wanted to see them fight because that's what would happen if Trey says one slick thing about Blair. He still has a punch coming for hitting Blair anyway. Nathan could feel his temper rising. He took a deep breath, he didn't need to lose it, not yet.

He didn't inform Blair about what was going on because he didn't want her showing up like he knew she would. Feeling a bit hypocritical, he grabbed his keys and headed for his car making the drive to Trey's. When he pulled up, he was impressed with how commendable the gated complex was. Shocked how Charlie would have gotten the girl out of here without being noticed, he pulled into the stall in front of Trey's apartment. He knocked on the door and waited.

Trey opened the door and quickly pulled him inside.

"Hey man, why you grabbin' me for?" Nathan asked.

"Because Charlie's men are around my complex somewhere and they were gonna shoot you."

"Shoot me? Why?"

"To get to Blair. All of this shit is because of her," spat Trey.

"It's not because of her. It's because of Charlie; he's a sick, sick man."

"I don't care, I just want my sister home."

"I understand that and honestly, I think you should let us help you."

"Help me? Ain't yo bitch done enough? She's the reason we are in this mess anyway!"

Nathan didn't say a word. He balled up his fist and punched Trey smack in the jaw causing him to stumble back. The two guys went at it, punch after punch, kick after kick until both of their faces and hands were a bloody mess.

"Now, now boys. Let's play nice," said a voice behind them, causing them to both freeze.

"How in the hell did you get in here?" yelled Trey.

"That should be the least of your worries."

"What does that..."

Before Nathan could finish his question, a bag was thrown over his head. He tried to fight them, but whoever it was, was twice as strong as he was. He felt another person come and grab his legs and then, he felt his body be lifted into the air. He felt the guys carry him out of the house and heard a van door slide open. He was tossed inside, hitting his head on something sharp. Nathan felt a coolness running down the side of his face and reached for his phone but realized it wasn't in his pocket. That's when he knew he was in over his head.

CHAPTER TWELVE

Blair had called Nathan what felt like a thousand times, but no answer. She was getting worried. Unsure what was going on, she got in her car with Jazmine and rushed over to Nathan's. The door was unlocked, which was unusual, so she let herself in.

"Go check it out Jaz," she said to her dog as she ran inside.

Blair stood in the entryway to make sure there was nobody inside. When Jasmine came back, giving her the all clear, she walked in, and looked around herself. Nothing seemed out of place; nothing was broken. She looked through his kitchen and noticed Nathan's phone sitting on the counter. Grabbing it, she tried to turn it on. It was dead. Running to his room she found his charger, plugged it in, and waited. After five minutes, the phone started to power on and she was able to look through it.

She checked his messages; no new ones but from her. She checked his call log and his last call was from a number that looked familiar to her. Grabbing her phone, she scrolled through her contacts and landed on Trey's number confirming the number in Nathan's call log was his. She called Trey, unsure why he called Nathan. She wouldn't get the answer to her question because Trey didn't answer, either.

Running back to her car with Jazmine by her side, she sped home, and ran inside, yelling to Eevee.

"What's wrong, Blair?" Eevee called out.

"Something is very wrong, Eevee. Nathan is missing and the last person he talked to was Trey."

"Trey? Why would Trey call him?"

"I have no idea, but I'm pretty sure it has something to do with Charlie. I think I need to go to the cops, but I'm scared Charlie will find out. I don't know if they will believe me or even help since I've waited so long to talk to them. What if they make things worse?"

"They shouldn't make things worse, Blair. Honestly, they probably would have handled it a lot better and Charlie would be in jail right now."

Blair cursed herself for being so hardheaded; she knew Eevee was right. She agreed that going to the cops would be her best option. Eevee set up a meeting with a detective Matthews at a coffee shop nearby in a couple of hours. Blair just waited impatiently until then.

When she arrived, she debated on sitting outside since it was a beautiful afternoon, but she decided against it just in case. The coffee shop was dog-friendly, so she walked in, Jazmine right at her heels, and placed her order. She took a seat in the back toward the middle of the cafe area. She could see both doors and had an easy exit either way. Now she just would just sit and wait.

Five minutes after her coffee arrived, she got a text from Eevee.

He's here. Black leather jacket and boots.

Blair watched as he scanned the shop and landed on her making eye contact. He walked in her direction. Jazmine stood, alert.

"Easy, girl. It's okay," Blair said, calming her dog.

"You must be Blair? I'm Detective Matthews," he introduced himself.

"Thank you for meeting me here. I didn't know what you like, or I would have got you something."

"It's no problem. I'm a regular here, they'll bring mine out soon as someone notices me."

Sure enough, the waitress yelled to the back for the Matthews special.

"So, Blair, what can I do for you?"

Blair told him the short version of the whole story; leaving Eevee out of it. He listened, taking notes, and nodding often. Blair stressed how scared she was for the lives of her friends since she came to him for help.

"How do you know your boyfriend is missing?" he asked after she finished.

"Because his car is gone, his phone is at home, and I haven't heard from him since yesterday."

"Could he be visiting family or someone out of town?"

"No, he's not. He wouldn't have left without his phone or without telling me where he was going. Besides, if by chance that did happen, he would have called me some way or another."

"Okay, I understand. Has he, Charlie, contacted you since you found out your boyfriend was missing? Like with a ransom or anything?"

"No, nothing yet. Do you think he will?"

"Honestly, I do. I don't think it'll be a money ransom, however. I think he'll ask for a trade-- you for them. And that's exactly what we will do. Let me tell you the plan."

****

Nathan came to, blinking profusely trying to get his eyes adjusted to the light shining on him and the darkness around it. It was hard for him to see past the brightness, but from what he could see, he was in some sort of warehouse. His arms were tied behind his back and his legs were chained to the chair he was sitting on. He couldn't see Trey or the girl anywhere. His mind started to race, how long had he been here? Was Blair okay?

Suddenly, a door behind him creaked open. He could hear two guys talking, unsure what was being said; he hung his head pretending to still be knocked out listening for clues. He heard them drop something making a 'thump' on the ground to his left. He listened as their footsteps started walking away from him. What he heard next shocked him so much, his eyes jolted open revealing a girl sitting on the floor in front of him, legs pulled to her chest.

Her hair was matted together all over her head, her face was bruised, lip busted. Her hazel eyes seemed frightened and worried. She looked at him, not saying a word. Knowing she heard what was just said too, Nathan needed to break the ice and talk to her. He needed her to trust him so he could figure out how in the hell to get them out of this mess.

"You must be Ebaleah. I'm Nathan, Blair's boyfriend. I know you heard what they just said, and I'm sorry, but I'm gonna need your help. I can get us out of here if you can untie me. Can you do that? Can we work together?"

Ebaleah said nothing, did nothing. She just stared at him as if he was speaking a different language. Finally, she moved toward him and untied his hands and began looking around for something to bust the chains from his legs. She found a metal bar and stood in front of Nathan whose heart was racing because if she missed the chain, it would hurt.

"Don't move a muscle," Ebaleah warned. "This won't hurt a bit."

A small smirk formed across her face as she raised the bar above her head, bringing it down with all her might.

Blair was at home pacing her living room. She didn't like waiting and she didn't like not being in control. She was trying to breathe in even breaths, so she didn't have a panic attack when it dawned on her that she hadn't once called to warn her parents. Yelling for Eevee to pull up cameras near her parent's house, she called her mom. Eevee had the feed up right as Blair's mom answered.

"Why hello Blair, how are you?" she asked all chipper.

"Mom, get Dad, and you two get into the safe room I told you to make."

"Huh? Oh, the safe room. We haven't gotten around to it yet."

"Mom!" Blair yelled. "Grab Dad and you two lock yourselves in a room, and I will send help."

"Send help? Sweetheart are you okay?"

"Yes mom, I'm fine, but..."

"Hold on, doll. There's someone at my door."

Blair saw one of Charlie's guys standing at the door, dressed in a FedEx uniform.

"Mom, do not open that door."

"Oh, honey, it's okay. It's just the FedEx guy."

"Mom, listen to me. It's not the FedEx guy. It's one of Charlie's guys, and he's here to get you."

"Why would the FedEx guy be here to get me?"

"Mom! It's not the FedEx guy!"

Blair watched as her mom opened the door and the guy rushed in, grabbing her with a gun pointed on her head. She watched as the phone fell from her mother's hand, hitting the ground. She sat frozen as the guy took both her parents out of their house and into a van and sped off. Dropping to her knees, she couldn't breathe; the tears were coming too fast. Jazmine rushed over trying to calm her; it didn't work.

CHAPTER THIRTEEN

Nathan closed his eyes, bracing himself for what could happen. He wasn't too sure Ebaleah was a victim after what he heard earlier. After several seconds of nothing, he opened one eye to Ebaleah standing in front of him smiling.

"Did you think I was gonna miss?"

"Honestly, I wasn't sure," he admitted.

She chuckled about to say something but quickly stopped as they heard footsteps coming down the hall. She hid the metal bar and sat back down on the floor. Neither one of them moved a muscle as they waited to see who was going to come in. Keys jingled then the door opened slowly; it was Trey.

"Oh, Trey I'm so glad to see you, I've missed you so much brother," she said as she threw her arms around him.

"Yeah, yeah, I'm sure," he mumbled hugging her back.

Nathan sat in disbelief as he watched what was happening in front of him. Could Ebaleah be in on the kidnapping too? Could this all be a big planned hoax to get to Blair?

Trey pulled his sister's arms off him. "Here's lunch. Sit down and eat it."

Trey dropped a bag on the floor and turned to leave. Nathan didn't move he just watched as Ebaleah grabbed the bag and came over to him.

"That was easier than I thought," she announced.

"Huh?" Nathan asked, confused.

"You didn't buy that sappy stuff, did you?"

"I mean, it's hard to tell which side you are on here."

"I'm on your side. My side. Blair's side," she said, holding up her brother's phone. "Figured we could use this to help us out."

"Wow. I can't believe you lifted his phone," he admitted, astonished.

"I'm not the same little helpless thirteen-year-old I was when they kidnapped me two months ago."

"Wait, you've been with Charlie for a whole two months? We *just* found out you were taken."

"Yeah, they came into my room late at night, woke me up by grabbing me, and pulled me out through a window. It was weird because my dog wasn't in my room like he is every night and he didn't come running when I screamed."

"Where was he?"

"That's a good question. He was lying on my bed when I went to sleep. He stays in my room all night, every night. I don't know what would make him leave. Unless someone he trusted already inside the house called him out."

****

Back at Blair's, she hadn't moved from the spot on the floor. Eevee had called Detective Mathews and was awaiting his arrival. When he pulled up and walked to the door, Eevee opened it. He walked in slowly, calling out to Blair. When he saw her sitting on the floor in a petrified state, he quickly ran to her side.

"Blair, are you okay?"

She didn't say anything. She didn't move or blink. He squatted down in front of her, placing a hand on her shoulder giving her a small shake.

"Blair, can you hear me?"

"She's in a state of shock, Detective."

"Who said that? Show yourself!" He demanded, jumping up pulling out his gun.

Silence.

"It's Eevee. She's my machine. You can put your gun away," Blair said, snapping out of her trance.

"Your machine?"

Blair decided it was time to let him in on everything about Eevee. She explained to him about how she got the house and how she found out about Eevee. Then, she told him about how she watched her parents get taken out of their house by gunpoint.

Eevee replayed the video that Blair watched, tears silently falling down her cheeks.

"Wow," was all Detective Mathews could manage to say.

Wiping the tears from her face, she said, "I just want Charlie to get out of my life. I just want him to finally pay for everything he's done."

"I'm not going to stop until we make that happen. I promise you that," said the detective as he placed a hand on her shoulder.

He told her about a plan he had in mind to flush Charlie out, but he had to confirm a couple of details before he could act on it. He also explained how they had an address for Charlie, and he planned on sending an officer to check out the residence. Before leaving, he asked if she wanted him to stay or if she would be able to make it through the night. Of course, she told him she was fine and walked him out knowing she was anything but fine.

Blair slowly walked to her room, legs getting heavier with each step. She plopped herself down on her bed face first. Crying into her pillow at first, then her tears became screams. She rolled over onto her back letting the tears run down her face into the pillow.

"I feel so...alone. I feel like I've been separated from my pack; like I have nobody," she said aloud to nobody particular.

"You are not alone, Blair," Eevee started softly. "You will get everyone back and Charlie will go to jail for good. Do not give up hope. You have overcome so much in your life to let him knock you down and take that away from you!"

Blair let what Eevee just said soak in. She could easily continue laying here crying; easily crying herself to sleep. But what good would she be to her parents, Eb, and Nathan if she was a mess? She sat up in bed quickly, thanking Eevee for what she said. Running over to her desk, she pulled out a notebook, planning of her own.

She first wrote down everything she had that could be used as a weapon should she need it. Then she started to jot down ideas on how she would approach Charlie. She stayed up all night long until her eyes would not stay open anymore; dreaming of the day she took Charlie down no matter what it took.

****

"Uh, can I help you?" Charlie asked, as two officers stood at his door.

"Are you Charles Anderson?" questioned the officer.

"I am. What's this about?"

"We have been made aware of a girl's disappearance and that she might be with you. Would you mind if we check around?"

"Not at all. Come on in. You won't find anything."

Charlie stood off to the side and watched as the two officers looked in each room of his house, the shed, and even the garage. Once they finished, they apologized for causing any inconvenience and left. Charlie jumped in his car and sped to the warehouse. He couldn't believe the cops showed up at his house. He obviously didn't hide deep enough. He knew it had to be Blair and her damn machine. Rage leading his body into the warehouse, he walked straight up to Nathan and grabbed him by the shirt, throwing him against the wall.

"What the hell?" Nathan spat out, confused.

"Your stupid girlfriend had the cops at my house. They went looking in every single room looking for that girl," he said, pointing at Ebaleah. "I'm pissed."

"What do you want me to do about it?"

Charlie saw red and began punching Nathan in the face and the sides. Caught off guard, Nathan took a couple of hard hits. Quickly fighting back, Nathan tackled Charlie to the ground, punching him in the face over and over. In rushed two of Charlie's guys, pulling Nathan off and holding him until Charlie could get up and continue the fight, unfairly. Ebaleah screamed and begged them to stop.

Nathan's face was a bloody mess, Charlie walked out of the room, knuckles bleeding, and his goons close behind. Nathan stood still swaying left and right slightly before he hit the ground hard. Ebaleah rushed to his aid unsure how bad his injuries really were and what she would do to help. He was barely conscious as she ripped an old towel, poured water from her half drank bottle onto it, and began to wipe his face. His nose was broken, blood pouring out of it. He had a couple bruised if not broken ribs, and the rest of his face was swollen and starting to bruise.

Jumping up, she ran to the door and started beating on it, yelling, "Charlie, you better bring him some ice. You really hurt him."

She yelled for a good seven minutes before giving up and going back to Nathan who was still out of it. She sat down in the fetal position next to him and rocked back and forth. Fear crept through her body; she could see how Charlie looked at her.

Nathan had stood up to Charlie several times in her defense, she couldn't bear to think of what will happen if Charlie tries now. She laid down next to Nathan's beaten body and closed her eyes, hoping sleep would come quickly.

A few hours later for some unknown reason, Ebaleah woke up. She looked next to her and Nathan wasn't there. She jumped to her feet, panicking looking around the room.

"Hey, calm down, sweetheart."

"Nathan, I thought you were gone."

"I'm here. I hope I didn't wake you. I am just hurting and couldn't sleep."

"It's probably best you're awake anyway. Does it hurt really bad?"

"Not horribly bad," Nathan lied. "I had a younger brother, and we fought a lot as kids."

"You had a younger brother?" asked Ebaleah.

"Yes, he died of cancer a couple of years back. That's how I met Blair honestly. She has his house. But, how are you handling this whole Trey thing?"

"Honestly, I really don't know. I just can't wrap my head around why he would do this. I mean, I get that he felt betrayed or hurt by Blair or whatever, but I don't understand all this. And what do I have to do with it all? Whatever his reasoning is, I don't know how I'll ever forgive him."

****

"Are you ready to bust out of this joint?" Ebaleah asked nonchalantly.

"Excuse me?" Nathan asked, unsure he heard her correctly.

"I've got a plan to get us out of here."

"How? We've been stuck in this windowless room for months."

She smiled and walked over to him explaining her plan. He couldn't believe how flawless it seemed. He couldn't believe that she was the one to think of a plan and not him. Before he could break down her plan, he heard footsteps coming to the door.

"Showtime," Ebaleah said as she bounced up walking to the door.

"Bathroom time. Let's go," demanded a stocky guy they haven't seen before.

"I need some women products," Ebaleah stated, without moving.

"There's toilet paper in the bathroom."

She laughed. "No, silly, I mean like *women products."*

The guy just stood there for a minute before he finally got it. He looked down, embarrassed.

"Uh, oh, yeah. Okay, I'll see what I can do. Wait right here," he said.

Nathan watched as Ebaleah smiled, moving a small piece of wood in the doorway just enough that the door wouldn't close all the way. Nathan's heart began to race. He couldn't believe this was happening. Would this really work? Could they pull it off without getting caught?

CHAPTER FOURTEEN

The plan was going so perfectly, Nathan couldn't believe it. He found a room that had a window he could climb out of and the drop wouldn't hurt him at all. He was about to start making his escape when he heard an older woman's voice he hadn't heard before. He listened closely and his heart dropped.

"Shit," he said out loud.

Rushing to the bathroom to find Ebaleah, he told her the plan was off.

"What, why would it be off? We are so close to getting free."

"Charlie has who I assume is Blair's parents. We can't leave them here."

"We can come back for them, Nathan! We can escape and bring help."

"But what if something happens to them in the meantime? What if Charlie gets pissed, we managed to escape and takes it out on them? Blair would never forgive us for leaving them with that monster."

Nathan had a valid point. Ebaleah would feel guilty if Charlie took his anger out on them and she knew he was crazy enough to do it, too. She convinced him that she would go get help.

"Okay, fine. You can leave and go get help. I can lower you down from the window in the room at the end of this hall. You can get help and bring them back to us."

"Deal."

"Just promise me that you'll be safe."

"I promise, Nathan."

Nathan led Ebaleah to the window and quickly lowered her down to the ground safely. He power walked to the room where they were being kept and shut the door. He prayed Ebaleah could bring back help quickly; he was sick of being trapped here. He couldn't imagine what was going through Blair's mind. She must be worried sick. Five minutes later, in walked Charlie, followed by Blair's parents. He pushed them inside then pulled the door shut and locked the chain from the outside. Nathan saw the absolute fear in Blair's mother's eyes, defeat all over her father's face.

"I'm Nathan. Are you Blair's parents?" he asked.

"Yes, we are."

"I'm Nathan, her boyfriend."

"It is so good to finally meet you, Nathan. Not under these circumstances of course, but we've heard so much about you," rambled her mom. "I'm Genevieve and this is my husband, Tony."

"It is so good to meet you as well. Once we get out of here, I would love to take you to dinner and really get to know you both."

"What makes you think we will get out of this alive?" questioned Tony.

"Well sir, there was a young lady trapped in here with me. She made a plan to escape and she's gone to get help."

Before anyone could say anything else, they heard the keys in the lock and in busts Charlie.

"Where the hell is the brat?"

"She went to the bathroom," Nathan answered playing it cool.

"She ain't in the bathroom. What is she up to?"

"How would I know? Your guy took her to the bathroom, and I haven't seen her since. That was just like ten minutes ago. I heard her ask him for some female products. Maybe that's what's taking her so long."

Charlie squinted his eyes at Nathan then ran out of the room, not bothering to shut the door. "Look for the brat, she's trying to escape."

"Still think we are getting out of this alive?" taunted Tony.

Nathan put his hands through his hair. He wanted this nightmare to end. He prayed to God who he wasn't sure was listening, that Ebaleah would be successful in bringing help. He couldn't stay here much longer, and from the looks of it, neither could Blair's parents and they just got here he thinks.

****

The day was creeping away before Blair saw the light for the first time. Rubbing her eyes, she didn't remember climbing into bed or falling asleep. Grabbing her phone to check the time, but it was dead. "Hey Eevee, what time is it?" she called out, placing her phone on the charger.

"It's noon," responded Eevee.

"Oh, man, I haven't slept this long in forever."

"You were up late and very tired. You needed the rest."

"You're right. Now I need a shower."

After Blair's nice long, hot shower, she made her way to her phone. She had five missed calls, voicemails, and three text messages all from a number she didn't know. She listened to the voicemail first.

"*Blair, it's Eb. I managed to get out. I don't have much time. I'm trying to get help. Nathan stayed back to keep your parents safe. I don't know where we are at, but I'm gonna send you a picture of the building. I'm gonna try to keep this phone on me in case you...oh shit, they are looking for me. Try to help us, please.*"

The line went dead.

"Eevee, can you do a trace on that number? Least figure out the closest cell tower to her location? Maybe do a search for this building too?"

"I'm on it!"

Fifteen minutes later, Eevee found a building that resembled the picture Ebaleah sent. Once she told Blair the address, Blair called and told the detective as she ran to her car. Despite his warning to stay home, Blair headed straight for the address Eevee gave her, fully prepared to save her family.

****

Ebaleah tried staying out of sight while she looked for anything that could help her: a car, a safe place to hide, the right direction to run. She saw what looks like an old shed and ran to it, shutting herself inside. She hid behind some junk under a table. Heart pounding out of her chest, she waited. Listening to Charlie's men yell, voices getting closer and closer to her location.

Someone opened the door and she held her breath, praying they couldn't hear her heart beating so loudly. She waited, hand over mouth; nothing happened. Frowning, she removed her hand

and exhaled. She still heard nothing, so she began to move from her hiding and came out face to face with Charlie.

"About time you came out of there," he said with a smirk on his face.

"Uh...I um..." mumbled Ebaleah.

"Save it, you little shit. You are becoming more trouble than you are worth. I can see why your brother got fed up and wanted to get rid of your pathetic ass. Looks like I need to teach you a lesson."

Charlie grabbed her by the ponytail, pulling her to her feet. He threw her up on the nearest table and held her there while he was looking for something to tie her up with. Threatening her if she moved, he let go and went looking in a toolbox, back facing her. Ebaleah wasn't going to just lay there and wait for him to do whatever, she jumped up grabbing a two-by-four and hit Charlie over the head as hard as she could. When he fell to the ground, she ran from the shed as fast as lightning.

Ebaleah ran and ran, but she couldn't find a way to escape; even outside the building, they were trapped. Wherever they were, Charlie had this place protected by an electrical fence that was three times the height of her. She stopped running; defeated. Tears escaped her eyes and tickled her cheeks before one of Charlie's men caught up to her. She didn't even fight them, she went willingly back inside.

"Eb, are you okay?" Nathan asked, rushing to her after they tossed her back in the room. "Did they hurt you?"

"No, they didn't. Charlie almost...well, I escaped from him. Nathan, we are trapped. This entire place is surrounded by an electrical fence tall as hell."

"Damnit. If only we could get in touch with Eevee. She could shut the power off and we could get free."

"My attempts at bringing help didn't fail completely."

"What do you mean?"

Smiling, Ebaleah pulled out the phone she lifted from one of Charlie's men. "I lifted this off one of the guys. I swear they are all muscle and no brains. I called Blair, she didn't answer, but I left a voicemail and sent her a picture of the big building we are in."

"You, sweetheart, are a genius!" Nathan hugged her and kissed the top of her head. "Now all we have to do is wait for Blair and Eevee to get us the hell out of this joint."

****

"Eevee, it looks like there's some sort of fence surrounding the area you gave me," Blair announced as she pulled up outside.

"Yes, I believe it's an electrical one with an alarm coded access. Let me see if I can't shut the power off long enough to get you in."

A few minutes later, Eevee came back with a plan that wasn't flawless, but would do the job. Before they could set things in motion, Blair's phone rang.

"Hello."

"Oh, baby. It's so good to hear your voice."

"Nathan, are you okay? Where are you? Is anyone hurt?"

"Baby, calm down. I don't have a lot of time. Nobody is hurt bad and I know we are on the second floor of the building Eb sent you a picture of. Have you figured out where we are? Can you send help."

"Yes, and yes. I'm already here with a plan to get in."

"Blair, don't you dare come in here. Just wait for the police," Nathan demanded.

"I don't take orders very well. My parents are in there. I'm coming in. The police are on their way, too."

Blair hung up the phone and told Eevee she was ready. Blair took a deep breath and waited for Eevee's okay to open the gate. Once she opened the gate and got in, she wouldn't be able to get back out until she either had everyone with her or the police arrived. She slid through the gate and closed it with no alarm going off. Scanning the area and seeing no movement, she made her way as quickly and safely as she could to the building that held all the people she cared about.

Back on the second floor, Charlie rushed into the room, mad as hell. "Which one of you worthless pieces of shit has a cell phone?"

Nobody said anything. Nathan slid the phone under some boxes behind him as Charlie made everyone stand up for a search. He searched Ebaleah last, being a little too friendly to her breast.

"Don't touch me," Ebaleah spat.

Charlie squeezed her breast with one hand and put the other hand around her throat. "I'll touch you if I want."

Nathan pulled Charlie off and punched him in the face making him stumble backward. Four of Charlie's men rushed in and forced everyone out of the room. Charlie told them they had to move because the police were on their way here. He instructed everyone to go into the van except Ebaleah; he wanted her to stay with him.

Ebaleah tried freeing herself from the muscular guy's grip, but he slapped her in the face. Lip bleeding instantly. Tony jumped out of the van and punched the guy in the face. Nathan took heed and did the same. Genevieve slid out of the van, grabbed Ebaleah and took off hiding behind some tall crates. She tore a piece of her skirt off to wipe Ebaleah's mouth.

There was a loud bang, and everyone froze. Someone had fired a gun.

"What the hell is going on here?"

"Nice of you to come back, Trey. Where have you been?" questioned Charlie.

"I've been out," Trey answered scanning the room for his sister." Where in the hell is my sister?"

"I don't know, but that little shit is giving me lots of trouble. When I find her, I've got to teach her a lesson."

"Aye, man, chill with that bullshit. She's still my sister."

"Oh, don't give me that shit, Trey. Don't act like you are some great big brother who cares about his little sister. If you cared about her at all, you wouldn't have planned her kidnapping."

Trey kept his mouth shut. One of Charlie's guys found where Genevieve and Ebaleah were hiding and brought them out, taking Ebaleah right to Charlie who instantly pulled her close and ripped her shirt open, exposing her breasts.

"I am going to teach you a lesson you will never forget," he said aloud as he walked off into a room. "Put everyone in the van and wait for me."

"Come on Charlie. Don't touch my sister," Trey yelled walking to them.

Two of Charlie's men stopped him, pushing him inside the van with the others. Charlie kept holding Ebaleah who was fighting to get free.

"Charlie stop," yelled a familiar voice.

Charlie stopped dead in his tracks and turned around slowly. Soon as he saw Blair standing there, a smile formed across his face. "My, my look who it is. How did you get here little Blairy?"

"Don't worry about that. I'm here. Let them go and I will take their place."

"I don't think so, Blair."

"Let Ebaleah and my mom go. Then you and I can get out of here. My car is parked by the gate, we can take that and leave. If we go now, we can leave before the cops get here."

Silence filled the room as Charlie pondered the idea. He was doing all this just for her, after all. His thoughts were cut short by the annoying sound coming from Trey's mouth.

"Man don't fall for that, Charlie. Don't believe anything that bitch says!" yelled Trey.

Charlie let Ebaleah go and she ran straight for Blair, crying as Blair wrapped her arms around her body. Charlie told his goons to let Genevieve go. Blair's mom walked over quickly too and embraced them both before her daughter rushed them out of the door.

Trey kept yelling how stupid Charlie was and how he shouldn't do it. Charlie walked over to one of his guys and grabbed his gun, shooting Trey in the leg. "Next time it will be a headshot. Know your place, Trey. I run this."

Nathan found an old rag and tied it on Trey's leg to stop the bleeding. He listened as Blair's mom begged her not to go with Charlie and watched as she pushed them out of the door. Blair locked eyes with him as she made her way over to Charlie. Nathan jumped up and ran to her, pulling her into his arms and fiercely kissing her.

"Your face," she said, tears running down her cheeks.

"I'm okay. Ebaleah took good care of me," wiping the tears from her face. "Blair, I love you."

"I love you, Nathan. I am so sorry I got you involved in all of this."

Before Nathan could say anything, Charlie tore her away from him and lead her into another room. He picked Blair up and sat her on a long desk as he caressed her face.

"I missed you so much, Blairy."

"We really need to get out of here, Charlie," trying to prevent what she knew was about to happen.

"It'll take the police awhile before they can get in here anyway. We've got time."

He ripped her shirt opened and began kissing her neck and chest. "Mm. I sure have missed all of you, Blairy," Charlie whispered into her ear as he pushed her down on the desk.

Pushing him off her, Blair slapped him in the face and jumped off the desk. Charlie wrapped his hands around her neck and begin choking her. It was getting harder and harder to breathe. Blair had to do something, or he was going to kill her. She could hear her Dad and Nathan trying to open the door.

Tony was beating on the door as Nathan was trying to kick it open with no success. Nathan dropped to his knees, hands still beating on the door pleading for Charlie open. Tony picked him up as police rushed into the building, telling everyone to freeze.

After six months, it was finally over. Police were taking Charlie and his goons out in handcuffs, and EMTs were checking everyone else out. They won. Charlie was going to jail for life, and everything would be able to get back to normal, eventually.

Both Ebaleah and Nathan were admitted to the hospital because of their injuries. Blair and her parents were all checked out and cleared, sitting in the lobby waiting to go back and see them.

"I am so sorry you guys had to go through that. I tried to protect you and I just couldn't."

"Baby, we don't blame you. This isn't your fault, it's Charlie's," said her mom.

"I know, but I feel slightly responsible. How am I ever going to look at Nathan or Ebaleah again?"

"They won't blame you, either, darling. Would you mind if I go talk to Nathan alone?"

"No, go ahead, Dad."

Tony walked in to Nathan's room. He lay in the hospital bed, eyes closed, but opened them when he heard someone come in.

"You mind some company?"

"Not at all, sir."

"How you holding up? They give you anything for the pain?"

"They did and it's helping. They said I'll be sore for quite some time, but I'll make a full recovery. I need to apologize to you, sir."

"Apologize? What for?

“Tony, sir, I am... I am so, so sorry. I failed you and your wife. I failed Blair. I am not worthy of your kindness, just leave me.”

“Son, this isn’t your fault. You almost broke your shoulder trying to bust through that door. She doesn’t blame you and you shouldn’t blame yourself.”

“I should have been able to protect her. I should have been able to prevent any of this from happening. She’s been through so much already. She didn't deserve this."

“And my daughter feels the same about you. She doesn’t think she should ever talk to you again because it was her fault all of this happened.”

“She has to know it wasn’t her fault. I don’t blame her, at all. I just want to make this better for everyone,” Nathan said, hanging his head.

Tony lifted Nathan’s head. “Son, Blair is strong, and she will get through this because we will help her. You will get through this because we will help you. Nobody blames you for what happened. Nobody blames my daughter, either. If anyone deserves blame, it’s Charlie. You are a good man and my daughter couldn’t be luckier to have a guy like you loving her. Now rest up so we can get you out of here."

"Thank you, sir."

"Call me Tony, son."

"Thank you, Tony."

Tony patted Nathan on the hand and walked out of the room. He was met by Blair who had been standing there listening in.

"Thank you for what you said, Dad."

"I meant every word of it, too. I really like Nathan. From what I saw today, he's earned my respect."

"That makes me happy. When you get home, promise me you'll get a safe room set up?"

“I will, my darling. I will. I am so damn proud of you, Blair. You saved that girl and your mother. You brought the police to save the rest of us. You faced your fears and you got this man put behind bars for the rest of his life. He will never hurt anyone again and that is thanks to you.”

CHAPTER FIFTEEN

Ebaleah was just told by the nurse she was cleared and could be released. She had just finished getting dressed when Blair walked into the room. Running over and hugging her tightly. "Blair, are you okay?"

"Yes sweetheart, I am. How are you holding up?"

"I'm fine. You have a great boyfriend. He looked out for me while we were locked in the room. I wouldn't have been able to make it if it wasn't for him."

"That's because he knew I'd kill him if he let anything happen to you," winked Blair as she kissed her on the top of the head.

"Blair, if you were me, would you forgive Trey?"

"Oh sweetheart, that is a tough decision and it's not for me to make."

"I know, but I just wanted to know what you'd do if you were in my shoes."

Taking a minute to think, Blair said down on the bed next to Ebaleah. "If I were in your shoes, I would go look into therapy. I would work on learning to deal with the anger and pain of what happened. I would learn to forgive him. Not for him, but for me so I don't let anger and fear control my life."

"Thanks, Blair. To be honest, I don't hate my brother. I really want to, but I just don't"

"And that is perfectly fine, love. You don't have to hate him," Blair said, as she led them out of the room.

Looking around the lobby for her parents, she saw them standing there looking back at her. Running to her mom, the tears were no longer able to be contained. She hugged her parents at the same time and whispered how sorry she was again. Her dad asked them if they were hungry and was off to get them something to eat. Ebaleah was in Nathan's room keeping him company.

"Mom, what am I going to do about Ebaleah? She has no family other than Trey. And she's under sixteen. I don't want to put her in foster care."

"She has nobody else at all?"

"Both their parents died when she was young. They never mentioned anyone else; no aunts or uncles or even grandparents."

"Since you aren't family, when CPS finds out she's been released from the hospital they will take her and try to find her family. If you tell them you are interested in seeking guardianship, they should be able to help you from there. You might have to go to court to prove you are financially able to take care of her."

"Whatever I have to do, I'll do it."

"I know you will, honey."

"She's been through enough in her life. She doesn't need to be thrown around from foster family to family."

Ebaleah came out and told Blair Nathan was asking for her. Blair took a deep breath and headed to Nathan's room. Looking at his face, made her heart break. His face was badly beat up; eyes black and puffy, lip busted, bruises all over. She hated how Charlie did this to all the people she loved and cared about.

"Hey baby, Eb said you were wanting to see me?"

"I did. I just wanted you near me," Nathan said, forcing his face to smile even though it hurts.

Touching his face, tears rolled down her cheeks. "Nathan, I am so sorry. If I would have known this would have happened, I wouldn't ever got involved with you."

"Blair, stop. None of this is your fault," he pulled her close to him, planting a kiss on her lips. "The worst part is over, and this will never happen again. You can finally live a life without fear of Charlie ever hurting you or anyone you love ever again."

"You are so right, Nathan. I can't imagine my life without you. Thank you for helping keep Eb as safe as you could."

"No need to thank me. I know how much she means to you. I honestly can't imagine my life without you, either. I couldn't stop thinking about getting back to you and how I never wanted to be without you again."

"I want you to move in," blurted Blair.

Nathan smiled. "I would love to move in with you, baby."

Blair climbed in the hospital bed next to him. "Oh, there's one more thing."

"What's that, babe?"

"I want to adopt Ebaleah. Or at least get custody of her."

"I knew you would, and I'll do whatever I can to help."

Tony walked in with the food followed by his wife and Ebaleah. For the first time in months, everyone ate and enjoyed each other's company without a care in the world. For the first time in her whole life, Blair wasn't afraid. She wasn't worried about Charlie or where he was or when he'd come for her. For the first time ever, Blair was at peace.

The next day, Nathan was able to go home from the hospital. He was still sore but promised the doctor he would take it easy and Blair would be there to take care of him. After he filled out all the release paperwork and changed his clothes, they were set to go.

"Hey, let's get out of here," Nathan said, wrapping his arms around Blair for support, and all five of them walked out of the hospital together.

Before they could make it to the car, a lady who was probably in her mid-40s dressed in a pantsuit with a clipboard, came walking toward them. Blair knew it was a lady from Child Protective Services and tried to prepare herself.

"Are you Ebaleah Daniels?" asked the lady, looking directly at Ebaleah.

Ebaleah stopped and looked to Blair who nodded. "I am."

"I'm Linda. I'm from Child Protective Services and I'm going to need you to come with me."

"But I don't want to go with you. I want to go home with Blair," said Ebaleah as she grabbed onto Blair's arm.

"And who is Blair? Your sister?"

"No ma'am, I'm not her sister. I am interested in seeking guardianship of her. She has no family and with her brother in jail, I would really like her to come live with me."

"Since it's Saturday, you will need to go to the courthouse Monday morning and file a motion for temporary guardianship in the family court. You will need to bring evidence that shows you can provide a stable and loving home for Ebaleah."

"I can do that. Is there any way she can stay with me until then?"

Linda asked to speak to Ebaleah alone away from everyone. When she agreed, Linda took her a few steps away and started asking questions. She asked all kinds of questions to make sure Ebaleah felt safe and staying with Blair was what she really wanted. After a good several minutes had past, they walked back up to the group.

"I understand you all have been through a lot lately. I will allow Ebaleah to stay with you for the weekend as long as you go to family court Monday and get legal guardianship."

"Yes ma'am, we will go first thing in the morning."

Back at Blair's, Nathan took Jazmine out while Blair got Ebaleah set up in a room. Her parents tried to stay at a hotel, but Blair refused to let that happen; she set them up in a room too and introduced everyone to Eevee. After everyone was settled in their rooms, Blair sat down on the couch and the emotions washed over her. She tried to stop crying before Nathan came back inside, but that didn't happen.

"Babe, what's wrong?" he asked rushing to her side.

"I'm just ...this is finally over, Nathan. I'm glad I can finally have Charlie out of my life forever."

They walked to Blair's room and crawled into bed, cuddling closely. Nathan passed out rather quickly, snoring. Blair, however, couldn't seem to fall asleep. She lay awake thinking about how scared she still was. She wasn't scared of Charlie anymore, but she was scared to go to court and face him and Trey in front of everyone as she retold what happened. She was also scared for Ebaleah's sake, not knowing how she would handle it. Blair figured the trial would last a good year or two because of her experience with the first trial that landed Charlie behind bars. She knew she was getting stronger but wasn't sure she could go through trial again.

Her mind would not shut off, so she began counting sheep. Twenty-five sheep later, she was deep in her dreams, her fears creeping into them. She began tossing and turning; sweat covering her body.

"Blair, wake up!" Nathan yelled, shaking her gently.

Sitting up abruptly, Blair's eyes darted open, "What's going on?"

"You were having a nightmare," said Nathan with sad eyes.

"Damnit, I thought I was done with nightmares."

"Baby, it's okay. You've been through a lot. These nightmares won't last forever. Let's get through the trial and you can put Charlie and these nightmares behind you for good."

****

Monday morning came quickly, and Blair was ready. She was ready to go into family court and walk out Ebaleah's legal guardian. That is exactly what happened, too. The judge thought Blair was not only a good fit as a guardian but was the perfect person to help Ebaleah through life after what happened and the trial. And Blair planned to do just that.

Blair thought Ebaleah was handling all of this quite well, but she wanted her to talk with a therapist to keep it that way. She knew how much talking with a therapist helps and so did Ebaleah, which is why she agreed to it.

Ebaleah was at therapy and Blair was helping Nathan pack his apartment. He didn't have a ton of things, but with the way he was moving, it would take them a while to get it all packed. Blair was packing the kitchen when he came up behind her, wrapping his arms around her and nuzzling his face in her neck.

"Hey, what are you doing in here? You're supposed to be packing up the living room."

"I know, I know. I just couldn't stand being away from you."

Turning around to face him, Blair teased. "Cause the living room is so far away."

"Oh baby, it's so far."

Nathan kissed her then picked her up and carried her to his room, tossing her on the bed. He jumped on the bed, bouncing next to her.

"I was thinking, we haven't got to have sex in my place yet. What do you say we do that before I move out completely?"

"Nathan, you haven't healed completely yet. I might hurt you."

"The only thing you could do to hurt me, is to deny me right here in my own bed," winked Nathan.

Blair pulled him close and kissed him passionately. They made love for hours, forgetting all about the stuff that needed to be packed. When they were finally able to leave one another alone, they hoped in the shower together. After some fun in the shower, Blair got dressed and headed to pick up Ebaleah from her appointment. She made Nathan promise to pack while she was gone. Kissing him bye, she skipped out of the apartment and to her car like she had never been afraid of being out of her house.

CHAPTER SIXTEEN

A year and a half later, everyone who was involved in Charlie's madness could get back to officially moving on with their lives. The FBI found enough evidence to put Charlie away for the rest of his life. Trey wasn't going away for life, but he would be in jail for five years for second-degree kidnapping; Ebaleah was satisfied with that. Blair was leaving her house more and the nightmares had stopped. The one thing that hadn't stopped since the day she got home from the hospital was the media wanting her to tell her story.

"Another reporter is outside," Nathan announced once he came inside.

"Seriously? They just won't give it up, huh?"

"The media is ruthless. They always want a story, no matter how hard it might be for that person to tell."

"I just went through this trial. I honestly don't know if I could go on T.V. and tell everything again."

"Maybe you don't have to," interjects Ebaleah.

"What do you mean?" asked Blair, intrigued.

"Well, instead of going on one TV station, I think you should write your story and mail it out to every news station! That way, everyone will see how horrible of a person he is, and you would be famous!"

"Eb, that is a great idea! I can even include your guy's experiences too!"

"I think that would be a great idea. I'll gladly tell you my experiences," exclaimed Nathan.

"Me too," chimed in Ebaleah. "Besides, you never know who you could help."

Blair ran and hugged Ebaleah. She was excited about this idea. She always wanted to tell her story, but never knew how; this was perfect. She rushed to call her parents, who were back at home with a top of the line security system, to see if they would be interested in sharing their experiences. They of course, agreed. Blair got off the phone, grabbed a notebook, and began mapping out what she wanted to say. After being lost in her work for a good two hours, she submerged from her room to the smell of something heavenly coming from the kitchen.

Walking in seeing the kitchen a mess, she busted out laughing. "What happened here?"

"Uh, well Eb wanted to make dinner for you and she doesn't know how to cook so I had to come in and save her," Nathan stated proudly.

"Oh, shut up, you know it was the other way around," Ebaleah exclaimed, hitting Nathan on the arm.

They all laughed, started making their plates, and then sat around the table enjoying small talk. Blair's heart was full and happy. She couldn't believe how great everything was turning out to be. The last two hours writing down her story from her first encounter with Charlie was very therapeutic. She hoped that if nothing else, she could inspire someone to stand up to their abuser in any way they could. She went to bed inspired and slept like a baby; no nightmare!

****

"Are you sure you want to do this?" Blair asked, pulling into a stall in the prison parking lot.

"I am. I really am ready to do this."

With that, both girls got out of the car and headed inside. They went through check in and a search, then were placed in the waiting room while the prison guards brought out the prisoners. They both saw Trey at the same time and Ebaleah squeezed Blair's hand. Blair squeezed back, giving her a smile.

Trey smiled at them as he took a seat. He looked different. He was more rugged and buff. His facial hair was long overdue for a cut or trim. However, despite his rough deminer, his eyes didn't seem as cold when he looked at them. That had to be good, right?

"How long has it been, Eb? Over a year now, huh?"

"Yes, it's been a year and a half."

"You look good. Growing up to be a beautiful young lady."

"Thanks. You look like hell."

"Ha ha. I guess I do huh, sis?"

"I didn't come here to laugh and joke with you, Trey. I came here to find out why."

"Why what?"

"Why you did what you did? Why did you have Charlie kidnap me?"

Trey put his head in his hands and sat there for a minute before he removed them and answered. "The answer I have for you will not make you hate me any less, Ebaleah."

"I do not hate you now, Trey. But I need to know."

"Okay Eb, I will tell you," glancing at Blair then back to his sister, he went on. "I was so pissed off with Blair and her machine, I started thinking about ways to get rid of the machine. When I found out Blair was seeing Nathan, I sort of lost it. I was so jealous that I wanted to get revenge."

"Wait, *jealous?* How could you have been jealous when you hadn't even given me the time of day for months?" asked Blair.

"I was falling in love with you, Blair. I was trying to come to terms with the whole machine thing. I didn't think you would start dating anyone else while I tried to figure it out."

Blair just looked at him, not wanting to give him the benefit of the doubt. Ebaleah didn't say anything at all, so he continued. "I looked up Charlie on social media and reached out to him. In exchange for helping me seek my revenge on Blair, he said he wanted to use you. He knew that Blair would do anything to save you."

"All that was so messed up, you know that, right?" asked Ebaleah.

"At the time, I didn't. I was just so angry I didn't care who I hurt. I understand now how messed up it was. I want to apologize to both of you. I understand if you never want to talk to me again, but Eb, I am so, so sorry."

"I don't know if what you're saying is truthful or not, and honestly I don't care. You have another four years here and by the time you get out, I will have grown and changed some more. I do not hate you. I am mad at you. I am hurt by you. I am going to therapy to work through what you did to me. You are my big brother, Trey. You protected me my whole life and I can't begin to understand the logic you felt at that time. I haven't yet, but I am working on forgiving you."

****

Five months later, Blair had completed their story. She let each one read it and they all loved it. She printed it off and mailed a copy to each big news station. As she dropped the last copy in the mailbox, she felt relieved; people would finally know all about Charlie. There was only one last thing she needed to do. With Nathan by her side and inspiration from Ebaleah, she drove to the prison that held Charlie.

She stood, head high, arms at her sides waiting on him to walk into the visitation room. Her heart began racing as she heard them getting closer. Nathan squeezed her shoulders and she took a deep breath as Charlie walked in, a smile on his face.

"Well, Blairy, this is quite the surprise. You must miss me as much as I miss you."

"Charlie, I don't miss you at all. I've let the world know what kind of person you are. You have taken enough of my life and you will no longer have a hold over me. I will leave my house freely knowing I no longer have to look over my shoulder. I am overjoyed knowing you will never hurt me or anyone else again since you will rot in your cell. I just came to tell you that I forgive you, Charlie. Not because you deserve it, but because I do." Blair walked out, Nathan close behind with a big smile on his face. They left Charlie in the visitation room with his mouth agape, astonished, never to see him again.

ABOUT THE AUTHOR

Jessica was born and raised in the small town of Coffeyville, Kansas. She first found her love for writing when her book about her dog and a tornado won a competition in first grade. She moved into writing poetry, winning an online poetry contest and still dabbles in poetry today. Her young accomplishments gave her the confidence to move towards her biggest dream: writing novels. Author of Try Me Not, she currently resides in Kansas City, Missouri with her boyfriend and seven-year-old stepson.

Follow her on
Facebook: @GrundyWriter
Twitter: @GrundyWriter
Instagram: @GrundyWriter
Blog: avoidingthebackspace.wordpress.com

Made in the USA
Middletown, DE
26 May 2020

96115981R00066